The

by Sharon Thompson

Print ISBN: 978-1-912986-02-6

Also by Sharon

The Aban

Also by Sharon Thompson

The Abandoned

For our Angel

Chapter 1

'What do you mean the bleeding has stopped?'

'Your Molly put her hand on me there now and muttered the prayers in Irish and that was that. You saw it yourself.'

I like this lady in the fancy coat with the fur collar. No-one other than Daddy thinks I'm much of anything. I'm supposed to look people in the eye and listen to their nonsense. But sure, all that just makes me tired.

'Does it take it out of you, Molly?' the tall lady asks me in her nice accent, as she moves to leave our kitchen. She stops in the doorway. 'You look exhausted now, child. I cannot thank you enough. You'll have to take something for helping me?'

'Are you sure it's stopped your bleeding?' Mammy asks the lady with the hair curls. Mammy's taking the wad of notes off her anyway saying, 'You didn't check? Are you sure now that it's all away?'

I peek at the lady as the whisper out of her is loud. 'Aren't ya a woman yourself? I know when it has all stopped. You shouldn't ask me those things with men present.'

Daddy slicks a hand over his remaining hair, leans back on the stool and thrusts his long legs out by the open fire and puffs on his pipe. I know that's the way he is when he's pleased with me. After the woman leaves in her big car, and Mammy isn't looking, he'll give me some sweets from the tin on the mantlepiece, that his eldest brother Vincent brought him from Dublin.

I don't notice the woman leaving as I'm away 'with the fairies', as Mammy calls it. There are no fairies like Mammy thinks. But, I suppose, I do go away into the shadows of my mind and listen to the dark shapes that I can see out of the corner of my eyes.

'I've told you time and time again, Nancy. Our Molly has the gift. And that educated woman left a grand stash of money.' Daddy fills his pipe with new tobacco and I sit on the floor, pulling the last of the stuffing from my straw doll's stomach. I roll it into little clumps. They are scratchy against my cheek. 'When God takes away something, he gives something in its place. Molly there is pretty and has the healing. They say as long as the child doesn't take money herself, she'll keep the gifts. We'll see over time how much of the healing she has. She could be one of the best around about here.'

Mammy pulls her dark curls back into the red ribbon she likes, and slops in the basin on the table, washing the best cups the lady drank from. 'I'd far rather that she'd be like the other children.'

'You should be grateful to the Lord himself, Nancy. Our Molly is a handsome child with thick red hair as anyone would be proud of. You can't have it all. I'm telling ya, we must be grateful for what we have. That doctor's wife there now said it herself: there's no point in us wanting what's not going to happen.'

'It's the 1940s! We should be moving away from all the old codswallop of cures and magic. My sister says the priest will not like to hear of it at all. You know Father Sorley is as mad as a bull when he gets the notion.'

'Molly needs to do this. 'Tis what they call her destiny.' Daddy puffs on, scratching the dark stubble on his neck and I smell the socks he's rubbing together in front of the fire. 'She has got to do it. 'Tis God's will.'

'Once the priests hear that she's performing miracles, you can explain it to them!' Mammy spits a bit when she's talking and her beautiful face crunches up the words.

'Are ya jealous of your own flesh and blood?'

Mammy opens the back door and flings the water into the backyard scaring the two scrawny hens that will die soon enough.

'Don't tell me that you're jealous of your own eight-year-old daughter? A child that isn't the full shillin'?' He is annoying her so she'll not miss him when he's out drinking porter later. 'She'll need something for a livin', as no man will take her on, despite the pale skin and angelic face. She'll need to be able to fend for herself because she's got nothing between her little ears.'

Mammy wipes her eye with the back of her hand and sniffs a bit. I can tell then that in the silence, she's staring at me. They both are.

'This next one better be all right,' Mammy mutters rubbing her big belly. 'Took long enough to get this far again. This next one better come out fine and talk to us properly and not be as odd as two left feet, like that yoke over there.' She's pointing at me.

I know they've waited a long time on this baby to come into Mammy. She used to say, ''Tis his fault. That thing between his legs is good for nothing. My Michael's not someone I should've married, but my family was in a hurry to be rid of the eldest, with another five daughters to sort out. I married beneath myself and I'm paying the price now. Don't be in a hurry to find a man. He needs to have working parts and not give ya a halfwit to rear, like this one!'

That's why Daddy asked me to rub his bits for him. Mammy and Daddy both wanted a normal boy and he asked me to heal between his legs. It all seemed to work fine, though, and I told him so. But he liked me to do it for him, and sure, I couldn't say no to Daddy.

'It's our secret,' he says.

I know it must be an unspoken thing, as it would make Mammy even more cross than she is already. Even I know that if she heard I healed Daddy's private place, she'd be livid. Daddy said his brother Vincent needed 'the healing' on his mickey too. I know Vincent's not married, so I would only do it the once for him, and he got angry.

'Them's for babies,' I told him as I heard the midwife talking to Mammy near the butcher's about making sure Daddy didn't wear his trousers too tight, or sit too long in the hot baths. And that she might get a boy if she walked around some big stones down in Carrowmore. 'You don't need the babies yet,' I whispered at Uncle Vincent and him at me to be his special girl too. 'You don't need the healing.'

He got wild angry and his mickey didn't work near me after that. I'm glad, though, he's off in Dublin now, as I don't like the air about him at all. Healing Daddy is different. I'm his blood and his favourite, special girl. I like it when he whispers how I helped him have another normal boy in Mammy's tummy. Even I know that the air about Daddy can be wrong sometimes.

'It's a gift you have.' Daddy's blue eyes are proud. 'Make me better, Molly.'

He is lots better since the baby is coming. Mammy's happier too – apart from when she is with me, of course.

'Mammy hates me,' I tell Daddy when Mammy puts on her good scarf and scuttles off to the bus, to go to her nearest sister's house. 'Mammy doesn't like me. I even taste the hate off her. She breathes it out at me.'

'She doesn't hate you,' Daddy says. I can always tell when people are telling me wrong things. Out of the corner of my eyes I can see the darkness around their heads.

'Do you see angels?' Daddy asked me last year when I was doing the healing on his mickey. Someone told him that the best healers could see angels. I know the nuns think that angels have wings and halos and sit in clouds or on our shoulders. They believe it, God love 'em. But, it's not right. I tried to tell them they were wrong about the angels, but they just took to beating me. So, I gave up.

People do have a sort of halo but there's no angels on their shoulders – there's just air. Maybe it's the angels making colours of the people's breathing? I call it good and bad air. People surround themselves in it and smell of it.

I always look around people and find out how their air feels. That tells me all I need to know and sometimes the shapes in the shadows tell me things too. They don't use words nor nothing. It's hard for me to explain. I know from the thumping Mammy did on me, that it is better now just to let it be and not talk about it too much.

It is best, for a lass like me, not to talk much at all – about anything.

'I see air, Daddy,' I told the only person who listens. 'But now that Mammy has a baby in her, you won't need the healing any more. I'll just heal your air by saying my prayers. I don't need to go near your mickey again. I'll sing to the air around ya, and make you better.'

'I'm a bad man,' he said as I held his head in my arms and touched his bald head and greasy hair.

'I know, Daddy…' I breathed on him and kissed his cheek.

'Heal me, Molly. Make me better inside.'

He was pale then, even Mammy said it. For days he was white as the sheets she made me fold with her. I know sometimes Daddy's air still goes bad but I hold his arm and breathe into his pipe and turn him good again. Mammy's air is always tight though. I don't seem to be able to cure her from anything, or make her love me at all. The creatures in the shadows tell me to leave her be. I try not to care about her insides or the heart of her.

I know most babies bring beauty into the world. All the women say it outside Mass when they touch Mammy's belly for luck. The thoughts of the baby make me so happy. The shadows have told me there's good things to come for me. Molly McCarthy will have better times… maybe the baby will bring them good things with him?

Chapter 2

'Take that pillow out from up your dress and stop that singing!' Mammy is shouting up the rickety stairs at me. 'I know you've got that pillow up your dress again when you're singing that fucking song! Do something useful for a change. Young girls shouldn't want big bellies and I tell you now, missy, DO NOT come home here with a belly to me or it will be off up the road with you!'

She still is as mad as a bag of cats. Daddy left whistling this morning and walked across the fields, to work at the Collooney train station, but I know she had words with him about money again. Then, I'd gone and made it all worse.

The girls in the village school where I have to go think that although I'm from out the country a few miles, I'm not that poor, cause we have a stairs that's just ours and my Daddy works for the train.

'We'll put up with you, if you keep telling us the secrets about the nuns and about the folk that pass in the street,' Treasa Byrne says as she flicks her nose pickings at me.

I know I shouldn't tell them anything and sometimes the shadows get cross with me for using my gifts, but it takes something for the other girls to play with me.

'Sister Augusta thinks the postman is handsome,' I laughed with the rest of them, 'and Father Sorely drinks.'

'We all know that!' Treasa shouted. 'You should go back to that small school where the one teacher thought you were the devil's child.'

'My mammy is going to have a boy,' I told them all this morning when things weren't looking good for me being included in the hopscotch. 'A boy.'

'You've been right about all the mammies and the babies,' Treasa said and came in close. I could smell the cream she says she puts on night, noon and morning, to stay good-looking. She needs that cream but it pongs something shocking. 'How do you know these things? Are you really a witch?' she asked and cackled an awful old laugh at me.

I know to stay quiet about the shadows telling me things, but I am no witch and so I whispered, 'No, I'm a healer.'

'Sweet Jesus?' She fell back a bit in her new shoes and looked scared.

'A healer is a great person,' Ellie McGrath said. 'You're nothing great!'

'Maybe I am. Cause like I know that… you stole Treasa's pencil.'

That's when all hell broke loose. We were thrown up before the Mother Superior. All for the sake of a few clumps of hair and a scrape of a nail on skin.

Mammy had been sent for there and then to explain why I was calling myself a healer again.

'Her father encourages her,' Mammy spat, and her looking all red in the face and grasping at her handbag. 'We all know she's an odd creature and you can all see that I'm doing me best with her. This school has to have her. No-one else will and I'm bet out with this baby coming and she just knows it. I can say nothing only… I'll have her father deal with this. I'm doing me best.'

There had been mutters of 'I know you are Mrs McCarthy', as I looked at the cold tiles and the nuns' shoes and the tear in Mammy's socks. She had her best clobber on, so things were bad and the air around her was seeping the hate out at me.

I had my hair wigged all the way to the gate and down the street for the benefit of everyone. 'I'm a good Mammy to you,

you… you… Little bitch!' Her lips were almost closed but she said it into my ear. I saw the eyes red in her head and I was so afraid. 'I know what you get up to. You're not the only one who can tell things. Healer, me hole! You are more like a she-devil that should be locked up or, I dunno, thrown in a ditch some place.' She wigged on at my hair. Her fingers tangled in it and she dragged me until her arm got tired and some clumps gave way.

She had to get the bus because she waddles with baby inside her. Then she had to pay. And, she had to sit quiet on the bus! This sent the air around her the darkest I've ever seen it.

I sobbed when we got down the big steps, knowing I was in the pit of hell. She had me all to herself on the quiet road and an empty home. She kicked me in the door and it hurt the small of my back. My heart was heavy in my chest, and my eyes pleaded with her to listen to me as she ranted on and on about her being a good, fertile mother and me being a bad bitch that must've been changed in the crib by the bad fairies. The shadows weren't with me and the loneliness was fierce, like Mammy's eyes. All was lost to me, until I thought of the baby that I helped put into her belly.

It was almost as if he talked to me through her stomach. He spoke without words, telling me to be still and calm and all would be right again. Mammy's voice was far away and she battered me with her fists a few times screaming at me, 'to listen.' Somewhere in the middle of her madness, I smiled at the baby.

That's when she lifted the twig-brush with the large handle and clobbered me about the shoulders. I fell over the chair and thumped my hip and elbow off the flagstones. The wood of the handle was hard but she couldn't use it well with her belly and the temper, so I escaped up the stairs.

This is where I sit now and listen to her yelling at me through the floorboards.

Daddy is due home soon enough and for once I pray he stops off for a pint (or four), so she doesn't make him hit me too. The anger isn't easing much downstairs as I can hear her banging the pots and the dresser's doors. The poor baby must be in a queer state inside her with all that badness, so then I start to pray that Daddy comes home sooner rather than later and we all get it over and done with.

Her feet are on the stairs now, as I hear the puffing of her and then she's in the room with me. Her socks are ripped more and the hatred dripping off her.

'NOT ONE excuse did you give! Not one reason for what happened. It's like you don't care!'

I'm on the floor now trying to get under the bed with its bad springs and she's stomping nearer with each word. 'Not one fucking care do you have for us. All you care about is Molly McCarthy. You won't even talk to anyone other than – himself. The great man of the house! The fecker who thinks you're the bees' knees and soooooo beautiful. Who made you beautiful? WHO? You, the wee bitch who burned the hole off me when you came out and ruined my innards so no other baby would grow in there, until now. This baby better be all right I can tell you! I can tell you here and now this baby better be normal. It's all your fault if it's not! It will be your fault! YOU who took the best years off me and you who doesn't give one shit about your mother who brought you to life.'

She's trouncing her fists off any part of me that she can find. Hailing the words out in wails.

I'm supposed to put up with it. 'Children must respect their elders and try to please them,' Daddy says.

I want her to die. I know it's wrong but with me pains, I just want her to die and leave me alone. The baby is suffering, I can tell. I don't know how I do it but I grab her wrist and pull it backwards. She howls. I hold her shoulder and drag her off me. Leaning on the bed her belly faces up at me. The angels tell me that the beauty of her is caked in tears and fear.

'Stop it,' I tell her. 'The baby. Please.'

The panting of her eases for a few breaths. I feel her nod as I can't look at her face again. I scuttle away over into the corner and sit on my hunkers and wait.

'You're always right, aren't you Molly? Always in control. All knowing.'

'No,' I whisper.

'And yet you know nothing at all. You know nothing! You're not able to read or write despite all the schooling you get. Two schools and not learning at all. Ya can only speak a few sentences! Won't look anyone in the eye either and hold your ears like you're doing now. You're just trouble for us all – that's what you are. Sweet Jesus we are tortured with you.'

'Sorry,' I mutter, cause I am sorry that I'm not able to reach her air and… make her stop.

'Sorry?' she asks. I can hear her shuffle up to sit on the side of the bed. The springs make a noise and she stares on at me. 'Sorry?' she says, slower this time. 'What are you sorry for? Making us the laughing stock of the whole county of Sligo? Are you sorry for having no sense of anything at all? Are you sorry for not being able to read and write or play like the other children? You're not normal. Are you sorry about that? No, you are not one bit sorry! What are YOU sorry for Molly, eh? Which shit are you sorry for?' She whispers the last line and I look at her. Despite her beautiful face, the air is tighter and coiled around her like a snake. 'You know, don't you, that he doesn't love you like he loves me? I'm a woman. His woman.'

'Who?' I mutter, thinking she means the Lord himself.

'You know who!' She's crying. I can hear her sobbing through the fingers over my ears. I don't know what she's on about any more. I just know if I say anything, it always gets worse. Much worse. The rocking I do also drives her over the edge of reason, but I must be doing it as she wails, 'DON'T FOR THE LOVE of GOD start that rockin'! Ya hear me? He loves me! ME! It was me he wanted until you came along. Me, who knows what you make him do. It's me who's carrying his child now. Me, who will survive all of this. Me, who won't be laughed at for being barren or bearing a halfwit.'

The good things the shadows talk about mustn't be coming, as Mammy's definitely the worst she's ever been. There's no sign of the shadows even coming to help me or tell me what to do.

'Sorry,' I say louder this time. It's all I know that might work.

She's standing over me and she stamps her foot and the floorboards make dust. 'You will be sorry. You sure will be fuckin sorry.'

Chapter 3

There is no word of me getting dinner even though I can smell the cabbage and bacon all the way up the stairs. There are loud voices but I cover my ears and fall asleep. Daddy didn't come to beat me. She will be queer cross with us both.

It is dark now and me awake and shivering from the bitter cold. The nuns call it winter and the men years ago, who tried to take 'the devils out of me', said it was the best time for all the badness to be stopped. The winter and cold kills off all badness.

I lie now shivering, hoping the Lord will make me die and make my life better. Treasa and the ones like her say that heaven's where they will go when they die, but that I'll go to hell with the demons.

The shadows tell me there's goodness in me and that brighter days are a-coming. They're always right. They might mean that I'd go to heaven now? Even though Treasa says I'll never go there because I'm not pure. I'll find heaven, though. I know I could get there when I try hard enough. I can make myself pure – whatever that is.

The shadows don't know what a 'halfwit' is, as they don't let me know what it means. I only get told what's important and that's not a lot sometimes. I know, though, that I must look out for a bearded man. A man with a nice beard will save me someday. I trust the shadows. They've been 'righter' than anyone. The shadows are not here now, though. No matter how much I squint my eyes down to the left and right trying to see them, they don't come. If there's a bearded man coming, where is he? Where is the something that must be bringing the good things? I know Jesus has a beard, so maybe that's who I am waiting on. If dying of the cold is what I have to do, then so be it.

The dying is taking a long time and the shivering is worse now. Even closing my eyes doesn't help the death sleep that folks talk about. I crawl more under the blanket in my clothes and whisper to the saints and the Lord himself.

Daddy wakens me.

He moves a curl and places it out on the bed. My long hair is never matted. That annoys Mammy too. She complains, 'She never needs to even brush it. Like some sort of magical child.'

He has the look that he wants me to do the healing on him. I close my eyes again and want away.

'It'll all be better when the baby comes?' he whispers. 'Won't it?'

I nod and keep my eyes closed tight as tight can be.

'What do you know about the baby? Is it going to be all right?' he whispers, and then we hear Mammy on the stairs. 'Just checking on Molly,' I hear him tell her, as he races to the door to have it ajar. He is pretending there's nothing in his head, as usual. I learn lots from Daddy about play-acting.

'She doesn't need anything. That biddy doesn't need us at all.' Her voice is full of anger.

I cry at that. The sobs make my hair wet and the mattress under my cheeks gets damp. Even me, who knows nothing at all, knows I need a mammy's love. The shadows come to hold me, they touch my hair and pat my shoulder, but it's not the same. Their little fingers run through my hair to soothe me.

They tell me that my voice is for me to use carefully and my gift is to heal those who need it, but I must save myself and my heart from the badness that's everywhere. I should shield my goodness and hide it deep inside me, then no-one can harm it or me. When the time is right, I will know what to do and when to use my few words.

I won't tell Daddy what I think I know about the baby coming. He doesn't care about what happened to me at school or the pains

I have from Mammy's beating. All he cares about is this son of his in her belly and the money I can make him for the porter. Sitting up tall on the bed, the breath of me is like smoke and the holes in my blanket get moved around, and that makes my feet stick out the bottom. Even in my boots, my toes are cold. I yank up the socks a bit, thinking it will help.

My little friends come to me. I see them down and to the right and left of my eyes. They sit and wait on me to notice them off to the side. They are in this world but they're not here as well. It's hard to explain. They are just forms of light and shade, but they tell me that I'm part of them too. My chest is heavy with the sadness in me but, slowly, with every swipe of their love through my hair, the tangles lift away. Inside me, they tell me that I am whole and will stay that way if I remember to heal myself. They tell me that no matter what, they will always be with me. But… they don't promise me much when I ask about the better days.

I ask, too, about how long these good days will stay. A day can be a short time or a long time. I know that better than most. A day of thumping and whacking from Mammy can last months and on the trains with just Daddy and me, they can be as quick as a blink.

My heart hurts even when I hold where I think it is. I feel it thump when I hold my hand there. I heal it as best as I can myself. I worry that when my udders grow, they will kill the goodness inside in my heart, like the udders killed the goodness in Mammy and all the others. There's no-one I know with them that's kind. There's no sign of the mounds growing yet. I have time and, sure, there's no point in 'going up to the meet the rain'. But there's something huge bothering me about the night.

Death is coming. I know it is. I pray that it takes me and hurries up about it. At least if I go to hell, I'd be a damn sight less cold.

My knees roll up to meet my chin and like the hedgehog Daddy showed me once, I stay curled up and pull my hair around my face to keep me warm. I can tell now that dying must not be coming for me, because it's a whole lot harder to die, than I thought it was. Thinking and willing it to happen isn't enough, as my eyes close in sleep.

It isn't the morning, but there's noise and then Daddy's shouting at me.

'Mind your mother. I'm off to get help.'

I go to the door of their room.

'Don't you dare touch me with those hands of yours,' she hollers at me from the bed at the far wall, when I peek in to see what's the matter with her. I know I'm not allowed in their room, unless I'm sweeping about the boards and lifting the piss-pot from under the bed.

I've no notion of going in any further. There's no want in me to touch her. I stay where I am and start my humming to clear the air. It drives her silly, but I know by the panting she's at that she's not fit to move off the bed. 'Stop that cursed humming! For Christ's sake! I cannot take the sight of you. I told him not to call you. I want none of you or those healing hands of yours.'

I'm happy that she's in pain because I still have the bruises from her. It's her innards that are hurting her, pushing the boy out too soon. The screams out of her are long and loud. I'm sure the neighbours up the lane won't be happy and it's the middle of the night. She's up on her knees, her back to me and her holding on to the railings at the head of the bed. There's blood on her nightie and there's more soaking into it. I could stop that, but I hum on.

'I'm going to die,' she says at me without turning around. 'It was all that annoyance from you today. You are the one who did this to me.'

The air is clearing in the room despite her bad chat and I stop my song. She's sweating in the cold, even the back of her lovely dark hair is wet. I wouldn't want to see an animal like her suffering, but there's little I can do.

'God, don't let me die here like this. The baby…' she whispers turning around. The pretty face of her changes to someone I don't know and she pleads at me. 'Don't let me die, Molly. Save the baby, please?'

I don't think she's ever spoken to me so nicely before. She beckons me to her and I obey. She holds my sleeves with her bloodied hands and pulls me into her. She smells funny and is all wet with tears, sweat and blood. My hands go to her belly, because that's where they need to be. Her breath eases and she leans on me. Her head leans on my shoulder and me rubbing the baby boy inside her telling him all the time with my soul, that it is going to be all right.

'That feels better. What you're doing is helping,' Mammy admits through her weak voice. 'I don't know what to do. I can't bear the thoughts of what's happening.'

'Dying ain't so bad,' I tell her. She grips my arms so tightly I think she will break them. She didn't want to really believe she was leaving this earth. I tell her, 'I knew death was coming, but I thought it might take me.'

She pushes me out from her but keeps a hold of my arms. Staring deep into my eyes, she begs me with every morsel in her, 'Don't let the night take the baby. Please. Save the baby.'

'I'll save him,' I say looking down at the swollen mass of him before he's truly living. 'I'll save the baby... But Mammy, I'm going to let death come and take you.'

Chapter 4

There's a whole lot of fuss when Daddy comes home with the birthing woman. They had to send out for the doctor because they were all too late in coming back. There's a whole lot of whispering about this and that.

The baby boy is out of Mammy. It came out as she fell forward on her hands in the bed. It came out of her arse. I knew to lift it, wipe it in the clean towel. I knew, too, to bite the cord that tied him to her and use the bread-knife. It was hard to do but the baby was breathing and as she lay back her own breathing got less raspy. I needed our baby boy away quickly from her, before the death came to take her soul.

'Little Molly probably stopped Nancy's bleeding,' Daddy is explaining to the birthing woman and Dr Brady. 'Molly's got the gift, you see. She stopped the blood. Why did Nancy die, though? Why's my Nancy not living?'

The birthing woman shakes her head and the doctor peels the baby out of my arms. He makes our baby cry. I'm crying, too, cause my face is wet.

'A child, though,' the doctor is saying. 'How did she know what to do?'

Daddy's hands are on top of what hair he has and he's looking down at the dead woman on his bed. 'She shouldn't have had to do anything. It all happened so fast. The poor critter. I left to get help. I thought I had time. It all came on her so fast. Nancy knew she was dying. She said it to me before I left, but I thought it was just the pain of it. Sweet Christ of Almighty, what's a man to do now?'

'She's got bruises on her face,' the doctor mentions and I see him staring at me, instead of Mammy and the baby. He's not sure what to think about me. There's whimpering coming from the naked little fellow who's back in my arms.

'His mickey's cold,' I tell the doctor and point at the precious little life Mammy left us. 'Mammy is gone with death now. We need to bury her before she starts to smell.'

Daddy starts explaining about me being a halfwit. I go to the drawer with the baby things that I know Mammy wrapped in tissue paper and start to cover the little fellow in the tiny clothes.

Dr Brady stands and says, 'Blessed be the life and death before me.'

The birthing woman is back with the hot water from the range downstairs and she motions for us all to leave the room until 'she cleans up'.

'I've got no teets for the feeding,' I tell the woman and she nods for me to go on out. The door clicks closed. Me and baby watch the men's backs go down the stairs.

Daddy reaches into the sideboard and his arm goes in a long ways and without looking his hand comes back with the whiskey bottle. He pulls the stopper with his teeth and takes two mugs in his fist from the dresser. The glug of the whiskey always makes me worry. He starts to make no sense when he's pouring whiskey into the mug and himself. The doctor's eyes haven't left me. They both are at the whiskey, so I snuggle the baby into me, until I see that I'm covered in blood too. The front of my dress, my nails and my wrists even. I'm dirtying the baby with it too.

'It's on your face,' the doctor says. 'Around your mouth. Did you bite through it?'

I know he means the gristly string that kept the baby tied to Mammy. I nod.

'And what did you say about the bleeding and her stopping it?' he asks.

Daddy's about to start on about that but there's a thumping on the door and the men in uniform step in the back door.

The paleness of Daddy goes whiter still and with them being 'sorry for our loss' and shaking hands. Myself and baby are ignored until the men go upstairs to check that Mammy's gone with death. They nod and do a whole pile of blessing themselves and saying what a great woman she was. There's a few questions about who was with her and what-not but no-one asks me much. Daddy does the explaining even though he wasn't even here and has no idea what happened.

'Molly is a bit simple. But she has the healing gifts. I left her here while I went for the experts. She's a great help to her mother and…' he stops and does a bit of a cough. 'She was a great help to her sweet mother and, for the love of all that's holy, has anyone any notion what happened to my Nancy?'

'Childbirth is a dangerous business,' a voice in the room says. I'm busy minding the baby soothing him with my finger and feeling his mouth suck around the tip of it. His dark eyes are wide and big like saucers in his scrunched-up face. His nose is like a button and his lips soft like his cheeks and chin.

'What happened, Molly?' It's the doctor's voice. What a clever man he is. I'm the one that knows.

'She doesn't speak much at the best of times,' Daddy starts but the doctor hushes him and asks me the same question again.

'It's safe to tell us, Molly. It might help to tell us what happened to your poor, sweet mother. Be good to let it all out now. You've been through a lot. Seeing that baby come out and all. How's about you tell us now what you saw?'

I can see her still in my head.

Mammy leans back on the bed and looks at me when I'm wiping the baby. There's no noise from her. I know she's bad now and she takes my hand in hers and she makes me look at her. Then with my hand in hers she puts it between her legs. I say my prayer and we stop the bleeding. The bed's full of her blood anyhow and there's more of her insides meant to come out, but they're stuck and anyhow it wouldn't make any difference. I take my hands from hers and cradle the baby into the towel. She didn't ask for him, but I gave him over and she lay back on the pillow with him all floppy and her the same.

He slips from her grasp a bit. I hold his bottom and put my other hand on Mammy's heart. She closes her eyes and whispers to me and the baby. She's frightened and doesn't want to leave him and Daddy.

All in the room now are waiting for me to tell them all of this. Even the birthing woman has her eyes on me. Daddy's gulping at the mug and I've the baby to swing in my arms like the women do. The doctor leans forward and takes off his fancy spectacles and I know by him he wants me to tell him all about it.

'She'll not talk at all,' Daddy's saying and the shadows are there yearning for me to stay quiet too. 'Our Molly won't know anything much. She never does. I've told you all that she's half-simple. Has us worried to no end about her. God is punishing me. Left me on my own to cope with her and a baby.'

I don't know if it is because the doctor's kind, or because Daddy's saying those things, or because I want the baby in my arms to think better of me, but I want to talk. 'Daddy's lying as usual,' I tell the doctor and then everyone else too. 'I was never a help to Mammy, until she knew she was dying.'

There's a glug of the whiskey from the bottle. I know Daddy's not wanting me to go on. I couldn't blame him. No-one ever wants the whole truth about anything.

'Mammy was never sweet to me.'

There's a gasp from the birthing woman.

'Daddy loves me more.'

'Shut up now, child,' my father says, but I'm walking around and cuddling our boy as he goes on. 'She's sad with the grief of it all and being here alone when the angel of a mother of hers died… Don't be listening to what she says. She knows nothing about anything.'

It must be the doctor's eyes that silence him. I don't know, cause I'm cooing at our baby.

'I have the power to stop the bleeding. But Mammy died,' I tell him.

'Do you know what death means?' I hear the doctor ask me. 'Do you understand that your mother's heart stopped beating and she's gone to heaven?'

'I knew death was coming,' I tell them without looking at them. The shadows stop me from saying what I really want to. I want to scream at them that I'm glad that Mammy's left me with the baby and Daddy. I want to tell them that Mammy had a tight and rotten heart and that all my healing couldn't cure her from it. The beings who look after me don't let me say any more. They won't let me say that it was me who stopped her heart and made her dead.

Yes, I held my hand on her tired heart and I stopped the blood. I felt it go slower until it stopped.

'I'll be your Mammy now,' I tell the baby. Dr Brady has something in his eye that he wipes away. 'Let's call you Jude.'

Chapter 5

The wake is bad. When people die more people come to sit with the dead corpse and tell stories. It seems silly, but it is supposed to help with the family's healing. I don't need any, though. I feel like a weight is gone from my belly too. The soul of Mammy is well gone now, and her shell is all beautiful, but starting to rot. I know she'll go to mush quicker than most.

All Daddy's men from the train yard have come and there's a lot of cursing and drinking, with the neighbours not staying long but leaving an odd tray of nice sandwiches and porter cake. Mammy would have been cross that the china cups aren't out and in ways I am too. My aunts and the women weren't for staying, either, with the 'hoards of brutes about' and someone stole the baby from my arms while I slept in Daddy's armchair.

'He needs milk,' Daddy told me when I pulled at his sleeve. 'He'll be back.'

There was something deep within me that knew he was lying to me. As I listen to the chatter, it's obvious that I might be given away, too, only no-one wants me. The creatures in the shadows tell me that a house full of men is not the place for me either. I freeze myself in the turf byre out the back of the house and fling hen dirt at the tin roof. I try to believe that Jude's sucking the udders of a nice Mammy.

The men teased Daddy about me being stupid and he didn't put them right. It stings me like a nettle burn.

'She didn't do much healing when it mattered now, did she?'

'Stuck with a child who's not the full shilling. Lord love ya, Michael. There'll be other women. You're young enough yet. But with the likes of that one burdening ya?'

I don't think of Daddy as having a real name. Michael McCarthy is a fine name. Mammy was called Nancy and her sister's called Aunt Bredagh. I hope they call Jude by the name I've given him.

There's an old sack from the coal that Daddy stole from the station. I get into it. There's no way I'm ever going to be clean again anyhow as there's no Mammy to scrub me or make me stand in the tin bath and hurt me with the nail brush. I make a bed for myself in the hard turf and hum a little lullaby for Jude. Living just makes me so tired. It is no wonder that dead people sleep forever.

There's one more long day of weeping and one more horrid evening of callers to the house. I slurp the tea a small woman called Jane O'Shea gives me and it is grand and sweet. She ruffles my hair and then wipes her hand in her apron. The bread's turning up at the edges but there's fish paste to lick off and that makes it soggy. I dip it into the tea and no-one gives out or notices. The priest does a great deal of throwing holy water everywhere and mutters, 'someone needs to wash that child.'

I know he means me, but people are mostly afraid of 'the child'. They say it to him in whispers. 'She's not right in the head. It might be catching.'

'She can't go into the chapel and her as black as the ace of spades,' Father Sorely says but no-one offers to clean me. Aunt Bredagh totally ignores him when he mentions it to her too.

I don't want to go anywhere anyway. They take Mammy in the long box up onto their shoulders. Daddy does a whole heap of sobbing and moaning. I laugh a good bit at that, until someone elbows me out the back door and shuts it with a loud bang.

When they're all gone, the silence in the house is nice. The room downstairs is still warm from the bodies and the open fire and stairs are clear of the sound of Mammy's footsteps. Their big bed is unmade and the window and mirrors are covered in case her ghost does something. My own room is as cold as snow and looking out on to the turf shed. There's nothing to do but sweep it with the twig-brush and empty the chamber pots. I'll wait on

Daddy and me to start living again without Mammy. I know I should be sad about her being gone, but I'm not. I'll wait to ask Daddy about me having Jude back.

I eat some of the picked-over sandwiches. My singing clears the house. I put some more fuel on the fire and boil the big kettle, thinking of the time Mammy threatened to cook me in it.

'I'll not fit.'

Then she'd mentioned the axe outside and making bits of me. On I sing until the water boils. I fill the basin and clear the table. There's plenty of water to soothe my swollen face and I swish a cloth under my pained arms and between my legs and the water is still clean enough to wash the few plates that I know aren't ours.

My one other dress that Aunt Bredagh made for me is getting tight but I squeeze it on and find a pair of Daddy's cleaner socks to pull up over my knees. I figure that the good days must be coming, but Jude's not with us and it feels wrong that he's missing. I pray that he doesn't go with Mammy. Some of the people said he might when they gathered around the coffin box.

Chapter 6

I know the car in the yard. It is the black one belonging to the doctor's wife. People say she shouldn't be allowed to drive. She is 'all over the road' and has been known to need someone to hill-start it for her.

But the lady with the fur-collared coat is back and smiling at me. Daddy has poured her tea. I notice it's in the chipped china cup that Mammy saved for herself. Mammy would've died of shame at this fine woman drinking from the chipped cup.

'I'm so sorry for your loss. I didn't come to the funeral as I was minding a special little man. My husband is the doctor,' she tells us. 'Dr Brady? You met him the other night.'

We all know who she is, but no-one says nothing. Aunty Bredagh with her dark hair in a bun and her brown eyes squinting, has warned me to stay quiet far too many times. I am to let them do the talking. They had hoped to bundle me off to wander to the river but the fancy woman had asked to see me, too, and they hoped that there might be more healing needed. Daddy likes the money.

'I was eager to come and see you again.'

She's talking to me, but I am looking at the fire. It's not blazing like Mammy would've had it for the visitors coming.

'Richard tells me it was you who named your brother.'

Her eyes are the bluest I've ever seen and she knows of Jude's name. I know she's in love with him too. I can tell.

'We kept his name. He's to be called Jude.'

My heart does a flutter. I hold a hand over my mouth. I might cry out that I want him back. I might scream at her that he is mine.

'Jude needs food and babies drink lots of milk and are hard work,' she says.

She's trying to make it all right that she stole our Jude. Took him for her own. The shadows are telling me that they sent her here. She was lonely when she lost her own baby. They tell me that Jude's cared for, that he is warm and safe and that she is a good woman. I'm not sure there's such a thing alive as a good woman. Even Aunt Bredagh can lash out at me.

'I felt I should tell you in my own way, Molly, that Jude is cared for… and safe… and loved.'

Her blue eyes search mine for forgiveness. I give it over to her with a smile. 'I know in my guts that I couldn't keep him,' I tell her.

She shakes her head and a tear lodges in the corner near her long lashes.

Daddy's looking for a drink even though it's only early morning. He's fidgeting with his boots and Aunt Bredagh's giving him the evil eye. The fire is warmer now and the flames lap the back of the hearth.

'You can come to see Jude,' she says. 'You can visit.'

Daddy's on his feet now muttering about it not being a good thing, but she reaches out and touches my arm. 'You saw him into the world, Molly. You can come see him anytime you want.'

I nod and look deep into the blueness of her. 'Are you who the angels have promised me?' I ask and she leans forward more in her chair.

'She's never mentioned angels to me before!' Aunt Bredagh blurts out. 'There's something not quite right about her, as you know. More nonsense comes out of her every day. Surely to goodness! She comes up with more play-acting all of the time. Pass no heed on her now. I told her to be quiet when a lady, such as yourself, was visiting.'

'Maybe I am the one the angels promised you, Molly?' She smiles. 'You healed me. It was you who made me well. No-one can understand how it happened. Maybe you do have the powers of the angels. You healed me so that I could look after Jude. There's a synchronicity in life, isn't there?'

I ignore her big words. 'The angels aren't all white with wings,' I tell her while staring into the flames. 'They are cross sometimes. The angels get cross. But they like you.'

'I'm glad.'

Then there's a silence a cart would take away.

'She needs lots of looking after. See all that chat there, it's very hard to listen to,' Aunt Bredagh announces with her pink cheeks, not that she's done anything to care for me. 'And this man here isn't fit to look after himself, never mind a child like this.'

'Molly and me are good together,' Daddy says. 'It's only been a few days. I need to get better at the cooking, but we'll get a way of working and set up a nice home now.'

The fancy woman looks around and smiles at me. I smile back. She's pretty. Not like Mammy pretty, but a niceness comes from her heart and her lips are fine and happy. I like that the shadows have found a tall woman with love in her for Jude. Her curls aren't natural, but her rosy cheeks are.

'Who else have you healed, Molly?' she asks me. Those blue eyes squint a little. I don't like her air suddenly. It changes quick as a flash. I'm not sure what I don't like about it.

'Why do you want to know that?' I ask at her, noticing she's got nice shoes.

'Do you heal all sorts of things? What else have you done for people?'

Daddy goes to answer, but a gloved hand rises from her lap and he stops.

'What do the angels let you heal, Molly?' she asks.

She sure likes my name as she says it all the time. The shadows like being angels but they know that there's some funny reason behind her questions too.

'There's no devil in me,' I say, remembering the time the priests came and doused me in buckets of holy water, held me down and prayed over me. It lasted far too long. It felt awful and me with no food. I peed in fright and it gave me the shakes for days. I was so scared even Mammy had cuddled me afterwards.

'Course there isn't a devil in you,' I hear her voice say. 'Why would I think there's a devil in you?' She's nice again, the sound of her true and the shadows nod at me to talk. 'Why would you say such a thing?'

'Folks thought she was possessed,' Bredagh says with a tutting and blessing herself. 'Nothing came out of her, even with the biggest and best of prayers.'

The lady's eyes go wide and her gloved hand goes to her mouth.

'I heal anyone,' I say wanting to bring us out of the bad memories that I cannot fix. 'I don't know yet what works and what doesn't. But your husband is the same.'

Daddy chuckles and sticks his hand into the dresser and turns his back on us all.

'And how do you know where it hurts or what to do?' she asks. 'How did you know how to help Jude?'

I love that she mentions our baby boy. Daddy or Bredagh haven't said a word about him, since he left us. She's asking me the question again as I've got loneliness stuck in my throat. I can't answer her. I swallow a few times and shrug. 'I just do what feels right.'

'That's her gift,' I hear Daddy mutter from the dresser. 'She's gifted.'

'Indeed,' the fancy woman says. 'And are you good at school?'

Bredagh laughs and it hurts my ears. I put my hands over them and rock a bit until I hear a muffled niceness from the fancy woman. 'It is fine not to like school, but you must go,' she says, knowing that no-one has made me go since Mammy died. 'You will go?' she tells me.

'Yes,' I lie to her. 'I'd rather be healing. I will never be able to read or write, but I know I will be a great woman.'

Bredagh is doubled over with the 'hysterics', as Daddy calls them, and the fancy lady's smiling at me, while Daddy takes another big mouthful from his mug.

Chapter 7

'**B**eing cross with me isn't going to bring anyone back,' Daddy says, trying to cook the potatoes. He keeps jabbing at them with a knife. 'I can't handle a baby. It's a woman's job and you're no woman.'

'Remember that then,' I say to his back.

He stops stabbing the hard spuds in the water. A few days ago he asked to see if I was growing udders but he could see plain as day that I wasn't. Even though he is almost always drunk, he is far from stupid. I'm tired of having no sleep and tired of living in the haze with the shadows. The shapes around me have been good to me, but they aren't real people. I need to stop depending on them for everything. Well, that's what they tell me.

'Jude's having the best of everything in that doctor's house. Them with no children an' all. The lucky fella will want for nothin' and he'll grow up knowing all sorts and having all that he needs. It's a lucky turn of events that she was here just days before... and that she took pity on us.'

'Pity is not nice,' I mutter. 'I want to visit Jude.'

'How many times do I have to tell you? There's no way of you getting all the way to Ballisodare and back. I'll be at work... and no good will come out of it.'

'She told me...'

'She pitied us and felt bad. That is all. She came to make sure we wouldn't ask for him back and got me to sign some papers. Clever doll she was. She came here when I was at my lowest. I had that Bredagh one breathing down my neck. I'd have done anything to make them all go away and leave me alone.'

'Us alone,' I remind him.

'There's no use in sulking. You're stuck with me and I'm stuck with you. We've to make the most of it. Going up to their house will make you want more and there's no point in that. Jude won't want to know the likes of us in years to come. You're only a curiosity to them, that's all. Once they feel you're not all that gifted, you'll be dropped like a sack of coal.'

He's afraid of losing me. I'm a burden to him, but he doesn't want anyone else to want or have me either. His heart is growing like Mammy's. Maybe the walls have some sort of bad medicine in them that makes us all go a bit wonky. Mammy didn't hate me when I was clean, pretty and quiet. But, she didn't want the other things in me coming out at all. Daddy was hardly ever here and he didn't need to deal with all of that. Now, he sees what she saw and he doesn't like it.

'I can make us lots of money,' I tell him to make the air change around him. 'Good days are coming.'

His air is a bit happier as he puts the lid on the spuds and checks on the meat in the pot on the griddle. It is black and smelling burnt, but he's still pleased with himself. 'You're a clever girl. Despite all those empty stares and humming, there's a pretty, clever soul in you. We'll be fine.'

'I told you, when I'm rich, it will be better. I'm going to be like St Brigid, or...'

He chuckles and doesn't help me. There aren't many women I can name that are known for being great women.

'I'm not going back to school. I'll make money instead.'

'There's no-one about here that will come to us for the healin'. Our luck is bad at the minute.'

'We could move?'

'Be gypsies?' he states like it is something awful. 'There's a roof over us here. There'll be no leaving these four walls.'

'I'm going to see the doctor, his wife and our Jude and you're going to take me.'

'No.'

We eat the spuds. I layer on the butter and salt cause he isn't caring. The meat sticks in my teeth and tastes like the pencil I tried to eat once. There's no more talk of school or the doctor's house. He doesn't make me eat the meat I leave half chewed on the plate. I wash the delph in silence and leave the pot to steep in water, like Mammy used to. I miss her when I copy the things she did. I ask the shadows to remind me that she was a good housewife.

Daddy always takes off to the pub at the crossroads when he thinks I'm sleeping, so I snore a bit to get him to leave earlier. I've hidden something in the turf shed that I need to check on and he's mad for the porter.

The little bundle is wrapped up, still weak and waiting on me. I hid it in a wooden box in the farthest, driest corner. It might be hungry and I take it out my half-chewed up meat. The black fur of it is warmer now and its little nose is wet. Its eyes open when I lift it and there are whimpers when I breathe into his little floppy ears. His paws are still limp and so I rub them and pray. My humming makes him snuggle into Daddy's old overcoat and we stay that way. I try to think of a name for my puppy.

The healing starts to work on the pup when I have time to take at it. The tiny tongue licks at the cold, hard meat and laps up the water I fill into an egg cup.

He was in the river with a bag full of his drowned brothers and sisters. The bag stank a bit but I poked about in the mess, knowing there was a living soul in there in need of me. It hadn't liked going back into the cold water for a wash and the shivering it did made me remember my own times of shaking.

'I'll be your Mammy,' I told it this morning and the shadows told me to take him home and say nothing about it all. The bag floated off on the current and we watched it leave us.

'I was sent to find you,' I whisper to the pup. 'We're meant to help each other. I've no teets for the milk, which is a curse, but let's hope me being your Mammy is enough.'

The little mite sniffs down into the scarf of Mammy's and I hum to the lump of fur and heal away at the air around the creature.

'You'll be my hound,' I tell the woollen lump in my hands. 'Like the Fianna had hounds. I'll need one too.'

The size of it now isn't big enough for wars or battles, but hadn't all the legends started with people being small and meek? There was a time when Grainne Mhaol the pirate queen was a mere girl and not let go to sea. Brigid, too, had been a young girl once.

'Let's call you Cuhullin after the warrior long ago. That's a long name. Let's call you Hull for short. Daddy might not let you stay, but I'll think of a way of persuading him.'

Keeping Hull is important to me, and there's no smell of death on him now. I'll probably have to tell Daddy soon, and I know deep down what I might have to do to be allowed to keep Hull.

Chapter 8

I must do something about telling Daddy about Hull, but as always I'm not sure of what words to use.

'If you don't go to school then I'll have the doctor's wife here again complaining,' Daddy says while puffing on his pipe. He realises then that I might like seeing her again. 'I won't have her here telling me what's what. We can't have them all saying that I'm letting you run wild all over the countryside. Be careful of that river too. I don't want you to drown!'

I might drown like the puppies. The shadows say that me dying would cure some of Daddy's problems, and they warn me to be careful. I must be quiet now for a time, but the heart stings inside me.

Hull's growing louder but hasn't made it out of the tall wooden box. I also bring in the turf so there's no need for Daddy to be near the shed. Hull's gnawing now with sharp little teeth and he's playful. It's hard to leave him, but he still snoozes in the woollen scarf, and while in the fields by the river, I tire him out for the early, dark evenings. Someone will mention to Daddy about me and a pup, but for now all is quiet. I fill Hull's belly full of spuds and milk and say a prayer over him to keep him sleeping soundly until Daddy takes off to the pub.

'The nights are colder if that's possible. You must be frozen in that back bedroom. We could move you down beside the fire in the evenings, back to the settle-bed?'

His bed is beside the chimney breast upstairs but the back bedroom is like an ice box. If I'm down here, I would be cosier. The settle-bed he talks of is like a big, wooden, curtained box with a thin mattress on it. I loved my settle-bed, which is why

33

Mammy got rid of it. I nod my head, but know that I'm walking into something that isn't as pretty as it seems.

'I'll pull in that bed, then, that Nancy made me put out into the turf shed. It's still intact and we'll make it up nice next to the hearth over there. Between the chimney breast and other wall? What ya think?' He points to the spot where it was. 'Old-fashioned and a wreck' for Nancy but where it was indeed my warm cosy bed. Daddy also fell into it when he came home full of whiskey and porter. When he didn't want to 'waken the beast in Mammy' and needed me to cuddle him instead.

'There'll be no room in it for you. I'm bigger now,' I tell him, standing as tall and as broad as I can. There's a smirk in the corners of his unshaven mouth. He has tried my blocked-with-a-brush door upstairs. He's rattled it just the once, since Mammy left.

'There's never much hurry on Michael McCarthy,' Aunt Bredagh says, so I'm surprised when he rises from his comfortable seat and suggests that I help him with moving it then and there.

'Wait until the daylight,' I tell him, as he sits again.

'You're right. Vincent's coming home for a wedding, he'll give me a hand with it.'

My boots, although tight as anything on my toes these days, let me sink my heart into them. I can see the swagger of that Vincent. He has far too much money in his breeches. He's over and back to Dublin looking for labouring men for his 'businesses' and women to 'whore for him', whatever that is. Mammy wasn't right about much, but she called Vincent a 'no-good-son-of-a-bitch'.

'When's he here?' I ask. From then, my days and nights will be filled with the fear of Vincent coming for me in the twilight.

'He'll be home for a good few weeks this time. He says he's brought some big trunks of fancy clobber home and we'll all look nice for the Easter fetes and the summer shows.'

I smile like I'm supposed to. I know from listening to the adults that Vincent and his pals have money and are vicious.

'I don't want to have to go near his mickey again.' I say it into the nice warm glow of the fire. That stays between us, and

Daddy sucks on his pipe and doesn't say anything. 'I don't want his presents.'

'You'll do as you're told. Vincent's a powerful man now. Made good in Dublin and he's good to remember us and to let us share in his good fortune.'

I pull at the thread from the sleeve of my dress. My knees are warming as I sit in front of the fire, but under me feels damp.

'You need to get out of that dress for one thing and those boots of yours are far too small. Vincent has clothes for ya. If you need to be grateful, you'll be grateful and be pleased about it as well.'

A tear drips from my cheek. I know he sees it.

'Nothing in this world is for free,' he puffs.

It isn't possible for me to be around Vincent for weeks on end. The thoughts of it will bring me out in hives.

'I'll bring death to him, if he touches me again,' I say.

I know the shadows have warned me to be quiet, but it's out now. Daddy chuckles and swings on the chair's legs. He's uncomfortable. The shadows tell me that Daddy doesn't like this. The shhhing is loud in my ears. But, I know that I'm powerful too, possibly more powerful than Vincent could ever imagine.

'I'm just putting my cards on the table.' I'm all high and mighty.

'Putting your cards on the table, are you now?' Daddy smirks on.

It was a saying that I heard Aunt Bredagh use about whether she would come to live with us or not. She wanted all sorts of things and Daddy had made it plain that her choices were few. Her husband had run off with some very young 'flousy' and left Aunt Bredagh high and dry with huge debts, a gaggle of geese and four boys to rear. 'The embarrassment at not keeping my husband was bigger than the pain of losing him,' she said, 'but I need a roof for my boys and if that means putting up with you, lazy Michael McCarthy, so be it.'

There'd been rumblings that she'd not been a proper wife to Uncle Matt for years. I could see how living with her and the noise from those big boys would drive anyone to up and leave! But I hadn't wanted her or her cards on our table. Daddy had mentioned 'the lack of space' and that he'd still go for a pint of an evening, and the boys would have to pull their weight and help about the place.

With me moving to the settle-bed, it seems likely that all Aunt Bredagh's demands have been thrashed out without me knowing.

'There'll be no chance of Vincent hurting me if Aunt Bredagh is here,' I tell the fire. I know Daddy's listening. His feet shuffle back and he leans in to tilt my eyes to meet his.

'You know so much,' he sighs. 'Did Vincent hurt you?'

I want to scrape out those stupid eyes of his. Does he not know that he's hurt me too? I can't answer the bad blindness in him.

'There'll be none of that ever again,' he says.

'We all know you're a bad liar, Michael McCarthy.' I sound like Aunt Bredagh when she says it.

The thump he gives me catches me on the side of the head. My teeth shake. My hand and side crash down on the flags right in front of the fire. The heat seers at me telling me to get up and away. I scuttle low and fast across the earthen floor and hide under the table. Through the legs of the chairs I pull in after me, I see his legs stretch back out in front of the fire. My rocking to and fro starts, and I hum to the pain in my head as the floor goes blurry.

'Nancy wasn't far wrong about you,' he says, not moving to see if I'm alive or dead. 'My cards are on the table now too, Molly. Bredagh and her boys are coming here and Vincent will be visiting. You will behave. Healing or no healing, we won't put up with you.'

The shadows must be lying to me too, because there's nothing good coming for me at all.

Chapter 9

There is no feet-smell of Daddy in the house when I waken up under the table. It's late evening, so he's gone to sup his fill. My right eye is closed and won't open. My jaw feels huge with my teeth a bit wobbly like the tooth fairy's coming. The taste of blood soon stops when I start my prayers. I hold my elbow, as I talk to St Brigid. The chairs aren't heavy but it takes me a time to move them with one eye not working and the other side of me aching. My boot has split open in the toe. I can feel the sole is slopping underneath when I try to walk. Bending to loosen the laces makes my temples pound like a drum. Instead, I drag that foot and wince when the other one makes contact with the ground. The fire is only embers, the room is as dark as the night around me. My friends gather my soul and tell me to be strong as I can be.

The sobs are loud from me and I scare Hull in the turf shed. He peeks but won't come out from the stacks of turf. I'd been slapping him to keep him from leaving the shed and now he doesn't know what to do. I'm outside as the rain starts to spit on me, clicking my tongue to urge Hull to follow me as I simply can't bear to lean down again. It feels like my whole brain might come out my eyes. My elbow doesn't hurt as bad when I hold it tightly. The turf shed starts to move in front of me. This shouldn't happen. I turn slowly to make my way up the lane. The creatures in the darkness help me to put one sorry foot in front of the other. I just want to fall into the ditch and die.

The neighbours' lights are out and the need for me to move in the other direction is huge, despite the agony I'm in. I'm almost at the crossroads that are the main road. To the right is

Collooney village, left is to Ballisodare, and on straight is for the train station. When I'm deciding which way to go, the fur of a warm Hull rubs up against my calf. There's whimpering and I can't look down much, but he's there. I get the will to move the extra yards to the sign on the road. When I reach it, all I can manage to do is lean my aching back to the stone wall next to the post.

The headlights of a car make me close my eyes. If I stood out into the road, maybe it might run me over and put me out of my misery? But, I don't want Hull to die and he's behind me. I wait for the car to pass on, but instead it slows to a stop. Daddy doesn't drive, so it isn't him. Whoever it is will more than likely tell him. I hear the car doors open and close again. Why did I walk into the night on my own when I had nowhere to go?

'Molly?' the voice asks me. 'Are you hurt, child?'

Father Sorely is not what I would call a kind man, but his voice sounds worried.

'She's been battered – again!' It is Dr Brady's voice. My good eye cries into the half-lit face of the handsome man and my lips tremble. Hull does a low growl but stays hidden behind my legs. 'You've been battered again, Molly?' he asks me, knowing the answer. 'There's no denying those marks, Father.'

Of course, the priest isn't sure if they should take me and Hull into the car. 'Her father couldn't have done this?' Sorely says as Dr Brady shushes him while lifting me into the back seat. I can hear the doctor is annoyed as he says, 'Being a parent takes more than a priest would know.' It shocks Father Sorely into a silence of sorts. Instead of talking to either of us he mutters prayers that I don't know, until Dr Brady leaves him off at his big house.

Through my one good eye, I can see the doctor is looking in a mirror. I'm used to a bus, but not a car. The movement is making my belly feel weak too. The leather is cool like face cream. Hull's nose rests on my knee and I hope he won't be sick in the car either. Sometimes Hull hoops up, even when there's no car jiggling. But, I just want to die or be far away by the ocean.

'We're almost there,' the kind voice says from the front. 'Jude will be glad to see you, Molly.'

Dr Brady has said both our names together. I thank my shadows for leading me up the lane. I thank them from the bottom of my stomach, but as I do so, I lurch all out of my belly. It spews down my front, over the seat and it plops onto the floor of the car.

'Not to worry, I won't stop now, Molly, we're on a bad bend. That's car sickness, I hope, and not the bash to your head. Stay awake now pet.'

'Sorry.'

'Just keep talking to me or hold those lovely eyes open just a little longer.'

I hum a tune to keep him happy that I'm alive.

'Who did this to you, Molly?'

He knows who did it, but he asks me again and then again, as I hum on. The healing is slow on myself. I'm so weak. 'Sorry,' I mutter again, listening and trying to see if my friends are near to tell me what I should do.

'Jude is doing well, Molly,' he says, and of course this helps my healing. 'He's getting stronger every day. We're delighted he's with us.'

'The angels led me to you,' I whisper as loudly as I can over the noise of the car. 'They told me to walk. I'd like to see Jude.'

He swerves the car to the right. I slide all the way over onto my side with the sway of the car. It stops and the noise of the engine goes off. I lie looking up at the doctor who's turned around in his seat, with Hull licking at my ear.

'I don't know what to say to you, child. We need to check you over.'

All around him, the air is fine. It's then that I notice his dark beard and I start to cry.

Chapter 10

I smell the perfume of the fur-collared lady in the long hallway as the doctor carries me in his strong arms. 'Hull?' I call.

'If you mean that smelly runt of a pup, he's under my heels,' Dr Brady says over me, as he kicks the door closed behind him.

'I'll walk,' I say, but he doesn't let me down until we are in a place that smells clean. The bench is metal and cold. He shines a small light in my eyes and holds my wrists. Then he pokes at my jaw and tuts over and over. He loosens my boots and I'm so grateful. I haven't taken them off for days, as getting them back on is more painful than leaving them be.

The smell of me must be bad enough. He wrinkles his nose a few times. I can't help but try to smile at him.

'You poor creature,' he touches my hair.

I lean into his hand with a sigh. Without thinking, I reach out for his middle and touch below his belt. I know Daddy likes my hands to go there when he cradles my head like that. Dr Brady jumps back from me and holds his groin and glares at me.

Tears fall and I wish they would stop. 'I'm sorry. I shouldn't have left Daddy. He'll be cross.'

Dr Brady doesn't move but stands there staring at me. My head hurts when I look at him. I close my eyes and hold my head instead. 'Please don't leave me,' I urge the angels. 'Tell me what to do.' Everything is strange now and I know that he's very angry with me, despite me trying to please him.

'Darling girl,' he says from a safe distance. 'What has happened to you?'

'A bearded man is coming to save me. My shadows told me so. I thought it might be Jesus.' Dr Brady is closer to me now. I slowly raise my tired arms to point at the wisps of his starting beard. 'But maybe it's you.'

I cry a lot then. Heap out sobs and even wails. I never did that before, even when I was alone in the fields or by the river. I screamed when there, until the neighbours complained to Daddy about me. But here, with him looking at me like that, I cannot stop my tired sobbing that vomits out with more porridge from my stomach.

He gives me something in an injection to calm me. I don't hurt as much. It stops me crying and feeling sickly. His soft shoulder carries me gently to a bed someplace warm. The sheets are cool but smell like lavender soap. I hear him cut and rip the dress off me as he whispers to someone else about 'finding me in this state on the side of the road'. I feel the air of the room hit my skin, but I don't try to hide myself as everything feels like it's going to be all right.

I don't want to give in to sleep and want to listen to the adult whispers instead. His wife's voice is there in the dimly-lit room and although my eyes are almost shut, I can tell that it's her.

'I'm here, Molly,' she says to me and sits on the bed. I wince as she holds my arm. 'Don't be afraid now. Your pup is in the kitchen. He should go outside but, like you, he is too small to be in the cold and dark alone.'

It hurts like hell to move.

'She's missing teeth,' the doctor tells her and she gasps. 'He hit her that hard, he knocked out her little teeth. Luckily, nothing is broken but that small jaw might be fractured. She's covered in new and old bruising. The poor little thing was like this the last time we saw her. But this is almost worse. It looks like she got a hard blow to her face and head! She's nine at the most, Violet. Nine.'

'Eight,' I whisper as that's how many slaps Daddy gives me. I thought Mammy made him do it; but maybe she didn't.

'This little, broken creature told me that the angels had sent her out in this state, on a freezing February night, alone on a dark road – to meet me.' The breath of him catches in his throat and he coughs. 'She said that a bearded man would save her. She thought it might be Jesus?'

A hand scratches across his hairy face and chin. I can hear it.

'That would break your heart, Richard. She thinks that you'll save her. She said similar to me. She asked me if the angels sent me.' Her whispers are far away now.

'What are we going to do?'

'We'll do what we must.'

My swollen lip doesn't let me say much, but I try, 'Please don't tell Daddy.'

I mustn't make sense as they come closer and ask me to say it again, but I can't.

'Your father won't know you are here for a while, Molly. Rest now, child. You must rest. We're here and you are safe in our home, Violet Cottage. You are safe now.'

'The good times are coming,' I tell us all and feel warm fingers run through my hair.

Chapter 11

The pill Dr Brady gives me helps the aches in my head but also seems to keep my friends away. There are no shadows to guide me and no voices in my brain. I try to hold my tongue and not let the doctor and his wife get cross. But my silence annoys them more, as they keep asking me things and sigh when I can't answer them. I rock a bit on the hard high-backed chair and hum to clear the air around us all. Jude is a joy to see, but I can't take him into my arms. They won't let me. The blanket I'm wearing might fall off and my arm is in a thing the doctor called a 'sling'.

I watch as the lovely Violet lady cares and fusses over our baby Jude. Mammy wouldn't like her. She's too proper. Mammy would've smiled at her and then would start giving out yards about her when she wasn't around. That was Mammy.

Violet pulls the little new clothes onto his tiny waving arms and legs. She kisses his button nose and speaks in a funny way to him. Would Violet smile at people and then curse at their goodness when they leave? Mammy's probably turning over in her grave to think that a woman like this has stolen her baby… our baby.

I like to watch her all the same.

They ignore my rocking and make eyes at each other as they eat their breakfast. I look about the room. Jude sleeps in the basket on the low, wide stool, and above him the window is tall and bright with giant trees outside. The mirror over the fireplace is as big as a window, but it's made of shapes. There's a sideboard with the good china in behind curved glass. Violet's back is to it, and the floor is soft like the pictures of petals that is on it. I rub my bare toes over and over the flowers.

'How are you feeling?' Violet tries for about the fifth time and smiles at me. 'We'd like for you to talk to us, Molly. We can help you. Your father will have to be told where you are, but if we knew what happened we might be able to help you all.'

The thoughts of Daddy stop my feet rubbing off the floor and my rocking starts at a fair pace. I can see him be nice to the fancy Violet lady and hear him grit his teeth like he does when Aunt Bredagh is around.

The walls of that house are making him worse every day. They throw out their badness into him. He's changing like Mammy. Or is it that she's gone and we've no-one between us any more? I pull my eyes in all directions, trying to see my protectors. But they aren't there.

'Molly!' The doctor almost shouts. Violet gasps and I jump in the chair. 'Time is short. Talk to us now, child. Who hurt you?'

'Mammy.' I pick at the blanket cause it's scratchy and annoying like his questions.

'Your mother is dead, don't you understand that?' He's trying to keep his voice kind. 'It must have been your father who hit you? Beat you so bad you were almost unconscious?'

'Daddy loves me more than Mammy.'

'Sweet Lord, help me,' he says from the far-end of the table. 'I told you, Violet, she doesn't understand what love is. She's been... Molly, do you want to go home?'

Violet reaches out her hand to stop me from ruining her blanket. 'Do you, Molly? Do you want to go home?'

'Yes.'

How do I tell them that there's nowhere else for me to go? There's no papers that they can get Daddy to sign to take me. Daddy's going to be mad as a bag of cats as it is. Here, I can see all the nice things Jude will have. His comfortable clothes and nice sleeping basket in this beautiful home with the nice walls.

'She can't really want to go back there?' Violet says. 'Molly, we could try to find you...'

But the doctor's off his seat and saying, 'Don't promise things we can't deliver. It's not fair on her. Father Sorely was certain there was little we could do. And if she wants to go home…?'

'Home to Daddy,' I say like I did when Mammy took me the odd time to Aunt Bredagh's. It's then in a rush I think of Hull. Daddy will definitely drown us both, if Hull's coming home with me, after all of this. Hull could stay with Jude. Dogs change their homes all the time. Like Jude, Hull is a puppy. He'll not mind. 'Hull, my dog? Can I sign papers for you to keep Hull with Jude?'

'She's clever in there after all,' the doctor sighs, sitting in the chair next to me. He smells of soap and tobacco and his beard is clipped in tight. 'We cannot keep the puppy, Molly. I'm sorry. But we will say to your father that we've brought him as a present for you and that we'll pay for his upkeep. How is that? Hull will live with you. We'll tell your father that you must visit here once a week to see Jude. I'll collect you and Hull in my car and you'll both come to dinner.'

Violet claps her hands over and over in a quick way. She's happy and something inside me loosens. A knot in my gut moves and lets me breathe a bit easier. My eyes are watery and my jaw aches as I smile at them both. Words come but they won't leave my throat.

Violet is all delighted. 'That's the best of plans, Richard! You clever man! We'll be able to… Molly, we'll know how you are and you'll see Jude. Your father won't have any trouble,' she mutters under her breath, 'or cause any more of it.'

Her words are so clear, I want to speak like her.

'What do you think, Molly. Would you like that?' the doctor asks.

'Yes,' I tell him and hear Mammy's hand clip off the back of my head and her yelling *Manners!* 'Yes. Please.'

Violet pats the top of my head. 'Let's get a bath, too, before you go… Let's get you a nice wash. I'll try and find you some clothes. Jane O'Shea in the kitchen has had girls. We will ask her.

How about that? Maybe when you come here next week, you could have another bath?'

I think the clothes from a stranger would be better than Uncle Vincent's Dublin clobber. I know if they make me go back to school I'll need proper clothes.

'Do you think Jude will grow up to be like Molly?' I can hear Violet ask Richard outside the kitchen when I'm in the big tin bath. 'I know you've got to see your patients, but if her father comes here, will you come back into the house and deal with him?'

I can't hear what the doctor says as the water moves when I do. The smooth bath is too nice to leave. I pretend to swim and Violet lets me stay 'five more minutes' at least five more times. I'm not good at counting, but I think it's five. It's only when I'm starting to worry about the tips of my fingers being washed away that I get out. They've gone all wrinkly.

Violet laughs at me and tells me, 'You must wash your hair.'

She suds it up and almost drowns me with jugs of cold water. It is even worse than when Mammy did it. My eye smarts a lot and my jaw's stiff but I take her hand and shake it as 'thanks'.

'You're so welcome. You can have your weekly bath here from now on.'

My jaw is on fire as I'm making the biggest smiles. The clothes are just the best clothes I ever did see. One even has a lace collar. I pick it to wear then and there. The under clothes are the perfect size as well and are soft as anything. I am not stuck into anything. They're just covering me like I see on other girls in school.

Violet tells me, 'Twirl around now. How pretty you are.'

I do look nice in the long mirror in the hall and I don't look at the big bruised forehead, chin and cheek. Violet wraps my hair in a towel. It then sits on top of my head while she shows me my nice new shoes. The towel falls and makes us both laugh, but the socks are like water as I pull them on. There's no itchy nonsense on them and I buckle my new shoes. Hull doesn't know me for a few moments when Jane O'Shea lets him into the kitchen. Jane is the small woman who made me tea at Mammy's wake. She looks different here in a white apron. But her brown hair and red freckles are the same. Her dark eyes cry when she sees me all dressed up. Her clean apron gets covered in her snotters but I'm too busy with Hull to worry if she's going to be all right. He's leaping and licking.

The sniffing he does at my knees makes me laugh out loud. I can tell that both Violet and Jane are happy to hear it. Both look jolly and plain Jane O'Shea asks, 'Will I make you more toast and sugary tea?'

'Of course, she'd love some,' Violet answers and she mentions some biscuits too.

Jude's basket is in the corner and Jane says, 'He's still sleeping sound. He knows he's safe.' This starts her crying again. I peer in at Jude and watch his chest heave and relax. A white feather floats and lands on his little chest. Reaching to take it, I whisper my healing at him and try to ease my own ills. I hold my 'slinged' hand in the air over him and quietly ask with every piece of strength I own that the saints and all of heaven watch over him when I cannot be here. The space around him and the women is clear and bright. These are the 'good times' the shadows talked of.

The tea is the best I have ever had and the biscuits are the same. I eat every one of the fresh biscuits they leave on the plate. Then, I think that maybe they were for us all. It being too late to put them back, I just stay quiet about it.

'Molly will be visiting every week, if her father agrees,' I can hear Violet tell Jane as I check in over Jude again. He's beyond beautiful. Hull thinks so, too, when I lift him up to look in on the miracle boy. It's then the shadows come and urge me to tell Violet that Jude will be a 'normal' child.

'He's healthy, Mrs Brady. Jude will not be like me at all.'

Violet looks grateful and Jane cries again into her apron.

Chapter 12

Daddy is like thunder. I can feel him in the doctor's house before I see or smell him. Father Sorely's with him, having taken him in his car. Violet is all in a dither asking about making the men tea as Jane has gone home to her own house. I'm standing by the fancy window wanting to pull up the sash and run anywhere at all.

'The child was lucky we found her,' the priest says, coughing but refusing to sit. 'Michael is here for her. He thought she was sleeping and he stepped out for a time. She's not the full shillin' as all the world knows. She ran off into the road.'

Daddy does look glad to see me despite his anger inside. His eyes are milky in his head. He peers at me past them all. I am still his special girl. The doctor has a bad air about him but that's cause he is angry for me. The shadows tell me to stay quiet and to wait. So I do as I'm told. The carpet flowers are nice. I can hear them all through the hands I hold over my ears.

'Michael is going to get his act together now. Aren't you Michael?' Father Sorley almost shouts. 'He wants to see his son an odd time, too, if you'd agree to that. He's not a bad man and he has the child's aunt coming to care for her.'

The shadows chuckle and nudge each other and I snort out loud. The priest loves Aunt Bredagh cause all her sons are altar boys. He rambles on about the luck I had after being hit by a car. The doctor doesn't say a word. Violet perches on the edge of a chair and holds his sleeve a minute as he pulls at his beard.

'Molly is to visit us here every week. She will see Jude. She has also taken on a puppy and we'd like for her to bring it with her too. We both want to see Molly often, and it will be good for her to have some time with her brother.'

I love Dr Brady there and then. He's even better than Daddy. I want to throw my arms around his legs and tell him that he's the best man in the world.

Daddy grunts and nods when poked in the arm by the priest. Daddy motions to me with his head. I obey and stand nearer him as he makes his way towards the door. He mutters a, 'Thank you and what day will ya call for Molly?'

It's arranged it will be a Saturday and that I might stay for the night as well. This seems to please Daddy. He'll have more time with the drinking. His face lights up and he reaches back to shake the doctor's hand. The doctor takes it, but his eyes are on me, as he says, 'We love having Molly here. It's no trouble at all. I will call for her every Saturday morning, bright and early.'

Father Sorley mentions, 'All girls are trouble and Molly will still have to go to Mass regardless of the house she's in.'

We're all out at the car before I realise it. Hull is thrust into my arms and we get pushed into the back seat. Daddy's in the front, his neck tight and the priest starts the engine. There's not a word in the car. Not one. Hull barely breathes and the shadows keep me company playing with my hair and telling me that Aunt Bredagh and the boys are in the house and that I will need to be strong now.

***

I ignore the tirade Bredagh starts at when she sees me. Her hair is in a red scarf and she's screaming that the place is full of my 'filth'. She's ranting about the pup and it staying in the house 'over her dead body'. I tuck Hull into the corner of my settle-bed and turn my back on them all and pull at the dirty curtain. It's falling down in one corner but it keeps me away from them all. Daddy's at the dresser, I can hear the plates clatter as he leans on it. Aunt Bredagh calls for turf for the fire. There's noise from the boys, but no-one troubles me.

I waken to hear Bredagh suggesting, 'They might keep her altogether? That Violet Brady is barren. And he's a man of medicine? It all looks bad for them. Even a halfwit like Molly would suit them. They might knock the healing out of her once and for all.'

Daddy's words slur. 'She's got a gift so she has. She's going to be a great woman. I know that in my soul, Bredagh. I shouldn't have hit her. It won't happen again. 'Twas worry and grief that took me off with them.'

Bredagh's not listening as she screeches to her boys to come and eat something that smells like cabbage. Hull sniffs the air but doesn't move and neither do I. Bredagh's shouting while battering the table with plates, forks and knives. The noise hurts my ears and my humming doesn't clear the air of her badness. 'Great woman, me hole!' she screams as she pulls back the curtain and demands, 'Get up and eat this dinner! I won't have that Dr Brady saying that you're neglected!'

Chapter 13

Bredagh's four boys don't bother me much. They're too busy starting their work labouring and being men. Like me, they just want to eat, sleep and stay away from the house and their mother. They are well liked in the village and it's odd that they are blood to Bredagh. She's a different kettle of fish altogether. Her torturing of me seems unending and she is always about the house. The settle-bed protects me from her and the badness in the walls. I curl against the wood and Hull and I protect one another.

He doesn't growl at her any more as I've had to train him not to.

'I'll poison that fucking dog,' she said.

I'm tired of her threats. This morning I said, 'I'll kill you if you do.' I didn't lift my head from my porridge. I know she heard me. For the rest of the day she left us be, but now I can hear her whispering to Daddy as he's home from work and by the dresser.

'Do you think she killed our Nancy? She threatened to kill me!'

I can't hear what Daddy's saying, but she asks him again. 'That one is a bad egg there, Michael. She needs to earn her keep or go to school. I can't have her under my feet with that mutt all day, every day. I have to work to keep this house. She's making more filth and annoying me with the sight of her.'

'Do you want every man and woman in the country coming here for her healing?' Daddy's by the table, the chair is rattling. He sits with a big sigh. 'But you're right she needs to start earning or doing something.'

'The turf shed out to the side of the house could be her healing place. There'll be no-one in the house then. We'll clear her a spot and see how it goes.'

Daddy must be agreeing, as she stops at the talking. I smell the stew she's good at making. She kicks the bed on the way past to tell me the food is ready. I'm not afraid of eating her food, but I do find it hard to eat when she's beside me slopping hers into her. Her air is so twisted. It is like Mammy's. There's no healing to be done on it and that breaks me a bit inside every day.

'It is Saturday tomorrow and the doctor came to the train station, saying his bit. He won't be taking the excuse that you're away with Bredagh again.'

Bredagh snorts and sits up all tall in her chair. 'He has some neck on him! All high and fucking mighty! Stealing your son and telling you then that he must see your daughter every week! The cheek of the bastard.'

Even Daddy is shocked at her cursing. 'It was you who said you couldn't care for another baby, or wouldn't look after it and sure I've to go to work. They have their reasons for taking him and I don't want to hear about it all when I'm at my dinner.'

The silence from her is welcome.

'Be ready to go visiting this Saturday and tell him nothing,' Daddy pokes my sleeve with his knife. 'Tell him nothing now, Molly. He's threatening all sorts, so he is. And men like him are dangerous. Think they know things about people, when they've no clue at all. You stay quiet, cause you've to come home and live here. I won't take a man like that knowing my business. He's feeling guilty that he won't take you on as well. They don't want a halfwit about them and that's the truth. But their conscience is bothering them. We'll use that moral nonsense in their heads and work them right. Do you hear me?'

I nod thinking Bredagh and Mammy have worked their badness into Daddy more and more, or maybe it does come out of the walls?

'We need more money to better ourselves. Bredagh and I are thinking of marrying. We'll be a family again then. They'll have no right to nothing and not be able to say things about us.'

I drop my fork to the plate and look at him. His baldness is complete now as Bredagh has shaved his head.

'I'll not want babies,' Bredagh says, but I'm still staring at Daddy. 'None at all,' Bredagh shouts. 'I'll take no chances on them being like this one. I've had enough boys. I'm not taking that Jude back either. Nancy's boy or not, I'm done with babies.'

'I'll not have to heal your mickey then,' I say at Daddy, but he's up and has me by the throat and off the chair. My feet dangle. I can't say another word. His blue eyes pierce into me to stay quiet and he loosens his grip. Hull growls loudly. Daddy lets me down gently onto the chair.

'What did she say?' the witch asks. 'What's all that about? What did she say?'

'Nothing. Nothing at all. Vincent should be here before long,' Daddy says starting to eat again. 'I told him I'd go to the village with him for a pint.'

Mammy would've hit the roof but if Bredagh wants to keep this roof, she can't go hitting it. Hull's nose touches off my hand telling me that he'll not let anyone hurt me ever again.

Chapter 14

Vincent hasn't changed. From the gap in the curtain on my settle-bed I can see him sitting at the table and winking at Aunt Bredagh as she pours him tea. His hip flask is silver now. He screws the cap off and on, like lightning. His large hands circle the china cup and his nose is huge over his moustached lip.

'You're as handsome as ever,' Bredagh coos at him. I suppose the eyes of him are bluer than Daddy's and he has lots of dark hair curls that she ruffles. 'Could you give some of them looks to Michael there?'

Daddy doesn't seem to mind that Vincent pulls her onto his lap. The laughs of her are fierce as she jokes about having the two McCarthy brothers for herself. She can have Vincent, but Daddy's mine.

I decide then and there that I will kill her. My soul hurts from killing Mammy, but the thought of Bredagh being gone would be worth the guilty suffering.

'And the doctor's coming to take the halfwit to visit the baby?' Vincent says and lets Bredagh off his knee with a slap at her arse.

'Don't talk. That fucker thinks we are shit on his shoe.'

The cursing of her is terrible and on she rants. Vincent laughs at her and they talk on about a doctor's wife needing to steal children from good folks. And about how I'm going to be such a disappointment to the Bradys.

Hull is beside me all warm and cosy. I love the smell of him as I lean back against his body and try to not hear them any more. Suddenly the curtain gets pulled back and there's Vincent. Hull gets up on his paws and it makes Vincent walk back a few paces. 'When did she get that?'

'Don't talk!' Bredagh is on her feet and she squints in at me and my Hull. 'Doctor gave it to her and will pay to feed it. Huh! He fecking better give you money in the morning, missie, or I'll poison that pup.'

I point at her and hiss like a cat.

'She's still touched then?' Vincent asks. 'Still no better?'

'Worse!' the witch says. 'Let's hope she behaves tomorrow or there'll be no doctor, no money, and no visits.'

Vincent winks down at me and smiles. My back gets a chill. The shadows urge Hull to growl and show his sharp teeth. I freeze to the spot. Vincent always manages to make me cold to the bone. 'You're getting prettier though, Molly,' he says. 'Growing up and you're clean? Look how fancy you look. I've more clothes for you all the way from Dublin. We'll give you nicer things than that doctor fellow.'

Hull growls a bit louder and I don't make him stop.

'That's one scary mutt to be sleeping with a child,' Vincent says, sitting back down at the table.

'Michael won't do anything about it. Says it keeps her quiet. And it does. She hardly comes out of that smelly bed and it suits me fine. I've work to be doing. I can't be bothered with her or that f-ing dog!'

'You're a fine woman, Bredagh,' Vincent says.

Daddy puts something on the fire and looks in at me. The eyes in his head are sad and full of pity and shame. How can he be so different from one minute to the next? There now, he is my daddy. He's not the man who held me by the throat and almost squeezed the breath out of me. There bending to add fuel to the fire, he is my daddy who loves me, but in the blink he's gone again and laughing at some awful joke of Vincent's and ignoring me again.

I can't pull the curtain as I just can't get the courage. Hull lies between me and them. I close my eyes and will the shadows to make it all hurry up to morning. They're drinking now. I hear Bredagh suggesting the dog needs out as it's farting.

Daddy comes over and touches my foot and gives it a waggle. 'Take him out,' he says.

We rush past Vincent and out into the cold night. The stars are spread out like a blanket over the sky. I ask them to go to sleep and make it morning. I want to see Jude and be in a nice house with walls that have goodness in them.

Chapter 15

When I open the car door, the doctor throws a smile at me through his beard. His spectacles are on and he pushes them up on his lovely, long nose. Richard Brady is what a handsome man looks like. I settle into the seat with a yawn. Vincent's snoring from one of the boy's beds in the backroom kept me awake. I couldn't settle at all, but I should have known that when he was sleeping he wouldn't be panting at me in the darkness.

I tried using my gifts from downstairs to make him die. I tried all night, but he's still snoring when I'm getting ready for the doctor.

Bredagh doesn't want to be up, but she made me terrible porridge, saying, 'I won't have them making out you're neglected and starved. Make sure to ask him for money, now. God, the head on me is lifting with the horrors of the drink. That Vincent is a bad influence.'

I hum to rid the memories of them from the car and the doctor asks, 'Do you like music?'

'I do.'

He starts to sing. I haven't heard a man's singing voice before. Not one that sounds nice anyhow. Of course, the men roar out the songs when they're drinking, but this tune is soft and wonderful. On and on he sings getting louder all the time. I don't want him to stop. I don't join in. The shadows poke me to try to sing but I don't and he stops.

'Keep singing please,' I say from the back. He glances at me in the mirror and smiles. His voice is just like… sweets.

'She likes my singing,' he says to Violet when she greets us at the car. 'And she wasn't sick. Look at Hull, he's grown in the few weeks and is well behaved.'

Violet holds my arm and pats it a few times. She rubs Hull's head but I can't look into her eyes. She's so lovely, I might cry.

'Jude is doing so well,' she tells me as she takes me into their lovely home. 'We're so glad you're here. Would you like some food? Are you hungry?'

In the kitchen, they both watch me eat. I try to do the 'manners' that they might like. Small Jane O'Shea is all delighted to see me too. I'm hopping inside with joy but don't know how to show it. I don't want to start snivellin' and cryin' into her nice tea and bread with dripping.

'Bredagh says that we need money for Hull's food,' I tell them all. 'Please?'

Violet is back in the room with Jude in her arms and the doctor nods his handsome face. 'They don't starve me, though. I am well fed. Sometimes, though, I can't eat as their badness makes things stick here.' I point to my throat. Jane makes a noise while the doctor nods. 'Sorry,' I mutter at them, because I am sorry.

'Don't apologise, Molly. You can say what you need to here.' Dr Brady is a fine, tall man. I wonder, should I tell him that I love him?

Jane nods at me and wipes a tear from her freckled cheek. 'This is your safe place, Molly pet. When you come here you can be happy... I hope.'

'These are the better times. The angels promised me some of these.'

Jane whirls around and mutters something to Violet that sounds like, 'She'd break your heart that child.'

Violet presents Jude to me, like he's a gift. I take him into my arms. There's no way to say how perfect he is; the lovely light weight of him, the softness of his blanket or the lovely sight of his wide, dark eyes and button nose. His lips are parted and they feel soft when I touch them. His cheek is like milk when I stroke it.

'Isn't he handsome?' Violet says all proud, like she made him herself.

'Yes, he's like Mammy. But, I know his soul is good. His blood is flowing nice and he's normal and healthy.'

Jane makes another noise at the sink and mentions, 'The whole place thinks you're a healer. Is it true, Molly darling?'

'Yes. Aunt Bredagh is setting me up like the doctor in the turf shed.'

Jane grins. 'Is she now?'

'And she and Daddy are marrying.' I sigh.

'Doesn't take them long to get things sorted, does it?' Jane adds.

'I think they aim to wait a bit,' the doctor says, throwing his eyes to heaven. 'Or so Michael told me when I suggested it was all less than proper.'

Jane clears her throat and mutters, 'That poor child and her mother hardly cold in her grave, and that aunt is some piece of work. I saw plenty of her at the wake.'

'Do you know my Aunt Bredagh?' I ask Jane's back and the plain face turns to talk to me.

'Not well, pet. I only know her to see. She's your aunt. I shouldn't say such things. I'm sorry.'

No-one has ever apologised to me before! Not that I remember anyhow. I'm taken aback. My words get lost in my head with the shock of it.

'Is she good to you?' Violet asks me checking that Jude's all right in my arms. 'Are you happy that they might make a family for you?'

'No,' is all that I can manage.

They let my tea go cold and allow me to hold on to the sleeping Jude for a long spell. They try to make out that they're having a normal Saturday morning around me. I keep myself to myself and cuddle Jude. Hull lies by the range and stretches out. Jude doesn't need any healing, but I whisper prayers over him to keep him safe and tell him that I love him more than life itself. I whisper, 'I won't die now because I've got you and Hull to love me.'

'Can I stay here tonight?' I ask out loud after a while. 'Vincent is home from Dublin and he's a no-good son-of-a-bitch.'

The doctor chuckles but Violet takes Jude back off me in a hurry, 'Such language! Don't say that again, Molly, now. That's terrible.'

'He's terrible!' I tell the doctor.

'When I'm on my rounds to see the lady at the big house, I'll pop in and tell your Daddy that you're staying until Monday.'

I race across to Dr Brady, fling my arms around his neck and tell him, 'I love you. I do.'

Chapter 16

Walking in my own back door on Monday morning is the hardest thing ever – until I spy an old table and chairs in the turf shed. They are in a place cleared of sods. It must be for me to meet with people for the healing. The door has even been put back on its hinges and there's a sign on it.

'Did you see your new place?' Daddy says, 'And if you look inside the settle-bed, there's new clothes for you and boots that Bredagh thinks will fit.'

It all does fit grand and there's no sign of Vincent. Bredagh's nowhere to be seen but I can tell she's not far away. The two dresses are second-hand. The coat seems new and the boots are barely worn. I'm delighted and mutter, 'Thank you.'

'I'm off to work and Bredagh's getting ready upstairs to go to her sister's like Mammy used to. She won't be going on Monday any more as you'll need someone with you for the healing. She won't be your mammy, you know. We just need to make things right and proper,' Daddy tells me. 'I'm hoping she'll be here to see to the people who'll start calling. Did you see the turf shed and the sign?'

'What does the sign say?'

'The Healer.'

'Jude's doing well and is healthy,' I tell Daddy, but he keeps stooping to tie his laces. He pulls on an old cap and overcoat. 'Keep the fire living for Bredagh and be a good child now.'

When he leaves, despite the cold, I want away from the walls and sit in the turf shed. I dream of people lining out the door and down the road.

It happens just as I picture it.

Tuesday morning, even in the mizzling rain, they stand lined out and down the road. Bredagh takes pity on some of the elderly ones and finds them a seat inside the house and sets an old pot out for their place in the queue.

For someone who can't stand lots of people, seeing a sick person one at a time suits me. They mostly don't talk. They sit on the stool and wait on me to hold their hand or touch their sore places. I don't ask them anything. I think they like that.

'Different from nosey doctors,' someone mentions as I touch her swollen throat.

There's some people I cannot cure, of course, and I'm not sure what to do about them. Bredagh says, 'Ask them to come back a few times anyway and we'll get a few extra shillings from them.'

There's no fee as such, cause an old woman told Daddy that I couldn't be charging like that or I'd lose my gifts. Bredagh tells them, 'It is what people can afford.' But Bredagh makes them pay what they can afford and then she squeezes more out of each one. I'm certain of that.

The guilt is huge when I see some people return who I know I can't cure. The lady with the large throat is back. Her eyes plead at me, as her husband tells me she can't breathe or eat very well now at all.

'You need to go to the doctor,' I tell them both. 'I can't help you much more. Try the doctor.' I think of my saviour and the best man in all the whole world.

'He says that there's nothing he can do.' The husband holds his wife's hand and she tries to breathe. I place mine over theirs. 'Then let us pray together. I'll ask for a safe and peaceful death. There's nothing I can do. I promise, though, that the kindest of angels will take you home soon.'

They let me pray with them. She doesn't cry or scream like she wants to. I hold her an extra few minutes and give her all the strength and peace that I can, as I rub her tired hands. She kisses my cheek and tells me, 'You're an angel yourself, sweet child.'

'Take care of yourself now and each other,' I say.

Bredagh, of course, is ranting at me over the dinner, having heard of my honesty.

'The woman is dying,' Daddy says, 'and sure the child must know it! People respect that she told them the truth.'

This stops Bredagh in her tracks and one of her boys says, 'The whole town's talking about her. Says she's curing all sorts.'

'I'm tired out,' I tell them, not that anyone cares. With a steady stream of people taking my soul every day, it is hard work. But no-one sees it that way. Hull and I love the river and we walk there in the early mornings before I start on my days. Mondays are busy after the talk in the pub of a Saturday and by Wednesday things are quieter. By Friday, Bredagh takes off to her sisters and I see a few folks who trickle along to see me and they leave their money under a pot by the back door.

I love my Saturday mornings. I am so grateful that the doctor's put a stop to them making me sit in the shed on a Saturday and Sunday. I sleep so soundly on a Saturday afternoon by their open fire in Violet Cottage. I often waken upstairs in the bed that's now mine. Dr Brady always asks me plenty about the people who come to see me. I can't explain to him how I know what to do.

'I dunno,' I tell him for the twentieth time. 'I just know what I know.'

'All right, Molly,' he says, but then he starts asking all the same questions the following week. He must think that I will have found the words to tell him. But I don't think I'll ever have them.

'Do you get any of the money?' Dr Brady asks me, and I shrug my shoulders. Bredagh tells anyone who listens that a child like me eats like a horse and takes a lot of looking after. They did buy me a new hat and gloves for the funny Mass that I go to with the doctor and his wife. 'Do you see what money people give your Aunt Bredagh?'

I shrug again praying he doesn't ask Bredagh about the money. She's more interested in it than anything else in this world. If he does mention it, she might take the head clean off him with her tongue.

'I just hope people don't take it out on you if you can't make them better.'

'I tell them if I can't cure them.'

'They accept it?'

'Yes.'

'What if they are not going to live?'

'I help them wait on the angels to take them home.'

'Do you tell them that they're dying?' His eyes are wide under the glass he pushes up on that lovely nose. 'Do you say to them that they will not survive?'

'Yes.'

'But how do you know this, Molly? That woman in Collooney stopped you and told you that her sister was gone and thanked you for giving her a safe death?'

I know who she means. 'The woman had a swollen neck. It was very bad.'

'But how can you just know these things? I'm a man of science and this makes no sense.'

'Sure, the world doesn't make sense,' I tell him and give Jude his rattle. 'I can always tell when death is coming. I feel it all over.'

'I see.'

'Like when Mammy was dying, I thought they were coming for me. I just knew Jude would be okay, but death was near.'

'You should go to school, though, Molly. A child like you should not be working and draining yourself like this every week. You need to be a child.'

'I can't learn schooling. I need to make up for what I did to Mammy.' The shadows are telling me to be quiet, but I need to tell him. I have to say it out loud that I am eaten away inside. 'I stopped her bleeding. I stopped her heart.'

The doctor takes my hand and holds my chin with his other hand. I can't look away.

'No-one could do that, Molly. Not even you. Your mother died in childbirth. It happens. You did not kill your mother.'

I know he'll never understand that the badness from the walls took me over then, but I won't let it happen again. Even though I want to kill Breedgah and Vincent, the angels won't let me kill again.

At least, I hope they will stop me. Killing people is wrong and I must not do it.

Chapter 17

The good times last for months and months. I'm happier than I have ever been. People from Leitrim and Donegal start to come to see me too. Word is spreading that I'm healing people of many 'ailments'. I'm also taking pain and grief away.

Hull is always with me and is growing huge like a hound should. Sometimes people pet him and ask if I heal animals. I tell them the truth. In time animals usually know how to heal themselves and they don't need me, but Bredagh has said to some folk to bring along their cats and dogs. I've even prayed over a parrot!

My Jude's growing and my stays at the doctor's help me with my talking. This makes me happy. Jane's hugs always crush me. Violet smiles at me on a Saturday and then her kiss on my cheek on a Monday morning keeps me alive all week.

People are wonderful to me – most of the time. I get an odd person who has bad air around them. I told one woman that I wouldn't touch her and she asked for her money back. I could hear her screaming at Bredagh who came to see if I was all right. One man tried to hurt me and Hull had to set him right about what's what. Mostly, I like the people who leave the turf shed.

'She barely speaks,' I heard a man tell Daddy outside one day. 'And yet you feel like she knows you inside out. She's an amazing girl.'

Daddy agreed and said, 'She'll be great woman, you know. She's got a destiny. I've always said it.'

'Aye,' the man said, 'I'd say you're right. Have you a gift of seeing things yourself?'

This was when Daddy took to telling some people's fortunes. It didn't last long as people saw through him. One man hit him so hard that his nose broke. My healing had stopped the bleeding, but I told him I'd bring it back again if ever mentioned fortunes again. He agreed and Bredagh warned him too. 'You don't mess about with those things, Michael. You won't get away with it. The fairies aren't something I believe in, but ya can't mess with it, all the same.'

'She does,' he said, pointing at me. The shadows told me that he was jealous of me too, like Mammy was.

'The doctor isn't jealous of me,' I said.

The thump was hard and knocked me off my chair again. All of my healing dried up the bruise but the swelling took longer to go down than I liked.

***

The doctor starts his questioning when I'm in his car. 'What happened this time?'

'I walked into the door.'

He doesn't believe me. 'Where was Hull?'

'In the settle-bed and it was quick.'

'Won't your angels protect you?' he asks me, poking my arm to tease me and try to ease his fears for me.

'They do help me. They found you, Violet and Jane for me. But best of all they gave me Jude.'

The days and months roll into years and Jude's schooling goes very well. He loves it. He never complains and I can't understand it at all. How can he be good at words and numbers?

My healing is bringing folks from many counties now. Bredagh takes a room for me to heal in, at the back of McLaughlin's pub in Collooney village. Bredagh's tired counting the money and Daddy's a drunkard when he's not working at the station. Himself and Bredagh never married and her boys grew up and are all away in homes of their own. As Daddy's beatings have stopped, I've to ask the doctor one day what age I might be.

'Fifteen, Molly. Sixteen on your next birthday.'

I know that I'm a fine lassie, as nearly every man and woman who comes to the healing says something about my beauty and height. Some mention my red hair. Men have noticed my breasts too. I do have a fine pair. I feared that they might take the goodness out of me, but they haven't. Years ago, Violet explained my own bleeding to me, with the doctor telling me, 'Don't stop that monthly bleeding. It's natural and will bring you your own children someday.'

Jude is a fine boy, tall for his age with big brown eyes and light-coloured hair. He's a good scholar who still wraps his eight-year-old arms and legs around me like he did as a toddler. We understand each other sometimes without speaking and this baffles the doctor's household. Jane is still making us sugary tea and telling us all the gossip from the village.

I love to hear her talk and drift off when she's telling me about the men who will romance me. She reads to me sometimes from her novels and we giggle at Jude pretending he's being sick at people falling in love. The shadows are still with me, but they say that I'm growing older and need to decide things for myself as well. They talk of even better days to come but that I may need to be careful and strong before those times happen. I try not to listen to the warnings they give me. I don't want to think of things changing, but I know deep in my gut that they will.

Hull is a fine dog but he is greying around his muzzle. He has never needed me for anything, even feeding him has become Bredagh's job. In fairness, she's fed him well with the doctor's money. I can't bear to think of him leaving me. However, something in my mind tells me he will leave me. I need to prepare myself for this, but again, I can't and won't think on it at all.

Chapter 18

The sun is splitting the stones on the pavement outside McLaughlin's pub. I work in their backroom and the line for the healing day seems done, when a man's head peeks around the door. It is Vincent McCarthy. Bredagh's on his heels. She is all in a flutter, as she always is when Vincent's around. Daddy is probably on the stool by the snug or at the station where he pretends to work. We rarely speak these days and I didn't know that Vincent was coming. But here he is. Him and his black mop of hair, sallow skin and the bad eyes on him. When he's about, I'm stuck to the spot as usual. His handshake makes my skin crawl.

'They tell me you're some lassie these days, Molly? Doing all sorts with these hands,' he rubs his own across mine. I swipe mine back. Bredagh can't hide her delight at seeing him or her disgust at me being rude to him. 'Be nice to your uncle, Molly McCarthy! Thank him for coming all the way from Dublin to see us.'

The cursing in my head is good for me. I do it over and over.

'Tell me…' Vincent asks me. 'Is there something you can do for me now that you're a woman of the world?'

Bredagh's not here now and neither is Hull. He's at home these days as he's not allowed into the backroom. I'm alone and the shadows aren't with me either.

'I'm told that you talk more these days. Full of gossip from up at the doctor's every weekend. Good job today's Thursday. I made a special trip down. I thought I would like to see you for a change. I think you should be nicer to me.' He pulls at my arm and manages to haul me into him. His breath is on my ear. Those hands fondle where they can. 'You've always been a fine lassie. I think you should come to Dublin for a while and make a name for yourself there too. I could look after you. Bredagh might come as well?'

His hands are on my arse and he is kneading it like dough.

I can't speak and can't tell him to stop. Nothing will leave my mouth, other than a cry. The tears are falling when Bredagh comes back in. He lets me go.

She's not stupid. She knows what he's at and of course it's all my fault.

'What are you doing? What are you at, you hussy? Your daddy's going to lose his mind, you throwing yourself at your own uncle.'

'Don't worry about it, Bredagh,' Vincent says. 'You know she's not the full bob. I'd worry, though, about what she'd do with some of the men in here. She might get a name for herself. And for you too!'

'Jesus Christ of Almighty! Is she at this with other men? Are you throwing yourself at the men who come here too?' Bredagh pulls at my arm to make me look into her horrid face. 'You're not whoring in here instead of healing? Are ya? It didn't occur to me at all that you might be at that.'

'Don't fret about it. Molly's always had an eye for me. We all know that she's only a slip of a silly girl with no brain at all.'

Bredagh sighs on about how looking after me for the past few years has been a torture. 'She's that quiet and sly…' They both laugh and talk about me as if I'm not human or listening to them.

I hum my tune to clear the evilness around me and bring my guardians back quickly.

'Stop that singing! Get out and into Vincent's car. Don't let her lay a hand on you, Vincent,' she says. 'I'll get Michael home shortly now, too, and we'll have the stew that I've had on since the morning. You behave yourself, my girl, and not a word to your poor father about this. We've a busy day tomorrow and then I'll go to my sister's on Friday. Mrs McLaughlin will have to mind things here.'

Vincent's hand is on my thigh all the way home, apart from when he changes his gears on the battered car he drives. He doesn't say a word and when we pull up at the house, I race to let Hull out of the shed. Hull doesn't even notice Vincent standing with his legs spread, in the backyard. My Hull is just so glad to see me. We race together for the river and to be away like we do. The sun shines on my face. I pray for all to keep bright and warm.

There is no-one awake when I let us back into the house. I lift the latch as quiet as you like. Hull's dinner is by the fire and dried up, but there's no sign of anything for me. There's no sound in the house, not even Vincent's snoring. Hull laps at his dish and makes my stomach growl. The pot is steeping in the basin by the door. I butter a crust of bread and watch the embers in the fire fade. Hull lies down. I sit into Daddy's chair and let my eyes close.

Sometime into the night Hull's gurgling sounds and gagging wakens me. Blood and bile is pooling from his mouth. He staggers to his paws and heads for the door. He's in a bad way.

All of my powers surface but nothing seems to be helping him. Outside, he keels over on the hard earth and he wretches to vomit. He peers at me in the twilight. He's dying and there's nothing I can do to bring him back. His innards are bleeding. I do stop the blood, but I know that even I can't stop the poison. There's too much damage. His breathing gets heavier. There are longer spells between each breath. I hold my hand on his heart and ask him what he needs me to do. I am to end this and how can I do that?

'Go with the angels my special friend. I love you. I do,' I tell him and hold the place in his chest where his love comes from. His heart stops beating. The gulps in my own chest make me heave out waves and waves of tears. On and on they come with 'Why? Why? Why?' I sit on my knees rocking over and back for a long while. Uncertain of what to do, I think of what happens to bodies when they die and lose their blood and air. I must find Hull a resting place. Somewhere near me, but somewhere safe for him now.

It's then I feel Vincent behind me. 'The poor dog must've got some poison by the river,' he says. I don't move or speak. Inside I am quivering. He chuckles a bit and walks back inside. The wheelbarrow wheel squeaks after I load Hull's heavy furry body into it. He's gone. I can't bear that his soul has left me here alone.

The shovel makes harsh sounds in the soft earth near the river bank. I can't breathe with the crying and the pains in me. Daddy's hand comes from somewhere and he takes the spade and finishes the digging. He's swaying a bit and his boots are untied, but he finishes the hole and motions for me to say goodbye to my friend.

I kiss the ears I rubbed at night to help us sleep, and touch his nose, and wipe his eyes. I whisper, 'You're the best friend I ever had and someone will pay for hurting your beautiful soul. Someone will pay for doing this.'

The sound of the clay going over Hull hurts my ears. I sing to raise his soul higher. 'Ave Maria, oh, listen to a maiden's prayer. For thou canst hear amid the wild, 'tis thou, 'tis thou canst save amid despair. We slumber safely till the morrow though we've by man been outcast. Oh maiden, see a maiden's sorrow, oh mother, hear a needing child...'

Daddy fills on at the earth. It covers my Hull's lovely fur and all goes black. Daddy pats the mound of earth down and catches his breath as I sing on. A hand leans on my shoulder. There's not a word spoken, but he knows what happened and is sorry for my loss.

But, as usual, lazy Michael McCarthy will do nothing about it.

Chapter 19

'I can't do the healing today,' I tell Bredagh. She's putting on her face in the small cracked mirror by the back door. 'Hull died and I've no healing in me.'

'Nonsense,' she says. 'Put on those boots and let's get moving. There's things to be done today.'

'I'm not going.'

'Your father's away to work even though he doesn't feel like it. Vincent has a few days off. You'd need to move your arse now if we're to make the bus into town. I don't want to cycle in the rain.'

'No.'

I've never stopped the healing, no matter how bad things are. Never stopped. I find peace and joy in helping others. The shadows come to me when I'm healing and I like the time I spend at it. Bredagh's struck dumb for once, and she doesn't ask me any more.

'Vincent poisoned Hull. Or did you do it together?' I ask the back of her.

Her shock seems genuine. But, she's meant for the stage, such is her play-acting. 'I wouldn't hurt the dog. I was good to that mongrel.'

She was. Hull was about the only living creature she was good to.

'Why would Vincent kill your dog? That's an awful thing to say,' she whispers and points up the stairs. 'He came home to see you. Why would he poison your Hull? He's got a great job and money. Throwing yourself at him one minute and accusing him of poisoning your dog the next? What is the matter with ya?'

I dare not tell her what Vincent wants. She'd be jealous. I know she would. She thinks he's all great cause he works in Dublin and wears a fancy hat that makes him look like an ass. I know better these days what he's after when he looks at me.

People have come to me asking me to heal their private parts, but I've never had to do anything I didn't feel was right. One woman told me of how her husband beat her and often pushed his mickey inside her. She needed some healing in her insides. I asked her lots because she had to come back a good few times after that. She said that she might just kill herself as no-one understood. The poor thing didn't always sense him sneaking up on her. Sometimes she was even sleeping and he hurt her badly. It sickened me to think of her alone in the dark with no dog to keep her safe and no angels to save her.

I spend the day sitting on Hull's grave and cry until I have no more tears. With no Hull to guard me, my friends tell me Vincent will sneak up on me. Sleeping that night isn't easy. I've only one night to lie awake for, as I'll be at the doctor's on Saturday morning and be away until Vincent's away on the train. I cry myself into the settle-bed and take the bread-knife in with me.

It's near dawn that I hear the stairs creak. Vincent is in the kitchen. Daddy's drinking is bad these days. He's out cold. Aunt Bredagh wears rags in her hair and they don't even keep her awake. I'm alone with the birds chirping outside.

'You know what I'm after,' he says aloud in the kitchen with no fear in him. 'A virgin like you is what I've been dreaming of.'

I grip the knife tighter.

'A fine beauty like you needs taking sooner rather than later. The horn on me is huge. There'll be no stopping the need that's on me, Molly.'

I hate that he can say my name and have no fear from what I might do to him. I swear to the angels that I'll stop his heart if I get the chance. I won't be weak and let him hurt me. He killed my Hull and he will pay for that.

He peeks in behind my curtain and my breath stops. His eyes are on fire, his grin large and wide. He's naked. There's not a stitch on him and his mickey is high and looking at me too. The brute sees the knife. It doesn't bother him. I slash it towards him but corner myself in the bed against the wood, with nowhere to go. He creaks onto the bed and gets nearer to me.

'Give me that knife now,' he mutters and waves his right hand at me and grabs at the knife with his left. In a second he has it from me. Despite my grip on it and the anger in me, he has the knife. I'm helpless. 'Give in to me now, lass. There's nothing you can do. Attention from a man like me is the best you'll ever get. Lie down there now and give yourself to me.'

I lung to get past him. In a blink, he has the knife to my throat. The heavy stench of ale is on my cheek and his hairy chest is against my arms and back.

'I'm used to holding my own, on the streets of Dublin. I fight with men for a living, Molly, there's nothing the likes of you can do to hurt me.' He grabs my wrist and pulls me out of the bed and bashes my tummy forward and onto the thin mattress. He yanks at my nightdress and pulls at me, panting and promising, 'I'll give you the fuck of your life. And don't you move or I'll cut you good and proper and even you won't stop the bleeding.'

I can't fight him. The weight of him is too heavy. Fear makes me freeze. I can't wriggle even. I don't move.

He's kicked my legs apart and his fingers are poking at me. I wouldn't even put my own fingers there. I cry. No sound comes out. There's a pressure trying to get inside me. It hurts and stings long and up into me. No sound leaves me. He thrusts and pushes and takes what he wants. He stops to breathe and 'enjoy it'. I sob into the blanket and smell Hull.

'Stop please. Make it stop,' I say in my head at least. 'I'll do anything. Just make it stop.'

He groans on and the burning isn't as bad. It goes on and on. He leans over my back and grabs a fist of my hair and pulls.

I don't know when he stops. I don't hear what he says. I'm away in the darkness. My knees buckle under me and I fall to the floor. He's not in the kitchen. There's no-one and nothing to help me. The shadows have their hands in my hair that's tangled from Vincent's fists in it. I push them off me and away. They were of no use to me when I needed them the most. I'm angry. Between my legs aches. My thighs are bruised. I can feel his finger tips and nails still on my side and legs. The pressure of him up inside me hasn't gone away. I can't even try to heal myself. I'm lost and almost dead inside.

Chapter 20

Bredagh bustles out earlier than usual to catch the bus, and either doesn't see the way I am or doesn't want to. Either way, I'm alone on the floor. The birds chirp on. I look at the ashes in the fire grate and everything inside me shrivels up. No words come and my tears stop. Then he's in the kitchen near the door, calling for me to 'make tea'.

The poison he used can't be far away. If I could just find that poison.

'There will be more nice times like that, if you're clever,' Vincent tells my back. I turn away from the noise of him. 'You'll need to get washed up. Your father will be wondering what's up with ya.' He touches my back with his foot. Every inch of me moves back from him.

I scream.

Loud and long it echoes around the place. I don't need to look to know he's pulling on his boots. There's a scuffle of a coat off the hanger by the door and he's warning me, 'No-one will believe the likes of you. A woman who can barely speak and me your father's brother. No-one will believe ya.'

Daddy is on the stairs. I recognise his footsteps, even though my eyes are closed. 'What's all the racket? Are you being silly over that dog?'

Vincent mutters, 'That's it. She's a lunatic, Michael! Took to screaming at me.'

'I'll ready myself for the work and then light that fire. She's not up for much today.' Daddy's back upstairs where the floorboards creak. Vincent is by the door lifting the latch. The air from outside rushes in to where I am on the floor. He stands a while, thinking of how to silence me further. Then his stale breath hits my ear, 'I'll kill your precious daddy if I have to,' he says into my hair. 'And everyone will blame you. I'll make sure of it.' His hand grips my shoulder. I howl again. Loud and long and piercing it startles him. I even scare myself.

'Shut up with that roaring!' Daddy calls as he races into the kitchen. 'The neighbours will hear ya. For the love of God, what's the matter with ya?'

Vincent is gone. I peer through my matted hair as Daddy shakes my two shoulders. I'm still whimpering like an animal that's been hurt, as he tells me over and over, 'It's only a dog.'

Hull was more than a dog to me. I can't find the words to tell him what's happening. There's probably not much need for me to say it anyway. If Daddy's mickey worked he'd probably want the same from me. Bredagh has told the women at the crossroads while we wait on the bus, that there's no need for Michael to worry her during the night. They'd laughed a bit that I couldn't heal people from the effects of the drink.

Daddy pushes my hair back. He tries to get me to look at him. 'Molly, it's only a dog.' My legs have no power. He lays me on the bed and tells me, 'Close your eyes a while now, child. Bredagh doesn't like Mrs McLaughlin knowing our business and taking the money on days like this anyway. Another day off won't kill ya.'

I can't answer him. My knees are grazed where they rubbed off my settle-bed. I know that there's worse than that in me. I am damaged beyond repair.

Chapter 21

I also know that Aunt Bredagh will come back and force me to get up. She'll not listen to any moans or groans and definitely won't hear a bad word said about the animal who...

She'll not listen. She never does hear me. This is too much for me to explain to the likes of her and Daddy. There are no words in me at the best of times for Aunt Bredagh. Daddy is lost to me.

Now that beast has taken... He's done his worst. What can Daddy do about it? What would he do? I know the answer is nothing. Like everything else, I'll need to gather myself and survive this.

'Heal yourself, you amadan!' Bredagh will spit at me. 'The boys never moaned. Thank God, I had boys. Why I took on a halfwit like you, I'll never know!'

I can hear her and see her say it, as plain as I can the ashes in the grate. The smell of Vincent is on me, fluid from him is on the inside of my thighs. His hands were tangled in my nightdress and in my hair. It's as if they are still there. His fingertips dug into my skin. He was in me and through me over and over. I can't move or think of it. I mustn't think of it.

Mammy wouldn't have helped me either. Father Sorley couldn't listen to the likes of this! Mrs McLaughlin knows men and their badness. But sure, I couldn't even wish her well on her daughter's engagement, so there's not much chance of me finding the way to explain this mess to her.

How could I tell any of them what he did? No-one must ever know. It must never happen again. Jesus, it couldn't happen again. Surely, it couldn't happen again?

Rising onto my grazed knees, I pray for at least an hour that he never gets to do this again. Ranting and panting out words I bargain with the angels, the saints and the Lord himself. I offer them my happiness, my soul, my everything, and last of all, I tell them to take my gift. This must never happen again.

The shadows listen. I can't see them, I won't see them. They let this happen. My battered life is broken. I won't hum or heal. I've pain inside that even I can't or won't touch. To fix it will mean it will go and all will be better. Nothing will ever be better again. Nothing will ever be healed.

I know I'm wailing like a banshee. I tear the nightdress off me. The curls in my hair that I can get at are hacked off with the bread-knife. I throw on my coat and take off up the lane, to the river.

The untied boot-laces make me stumble and take me out of my daze. I just want to get away. The river's running wild, the flow full and fast. The edges are shallow and the pebbles smooth on the soles of my feet. I slip in and let the coat float up and out. The water cleanses my skin and eases my bruises. The icy fingers ask me to go deeper, to lunge out to where I would be washed down stream, where I would drown and be away from…

It's then I hear a voice in my ear, as strong as a human whisper. 'No, Molly. No.'

I swing around. There's no-one there as I watch the trees and swaying grasses. The coat is holding me down now, sodden it clings to my legs and back. I'm cold and shivering, inside and out, but the shadows are murmuring that I'm cleaned of him and that they will help me. Ignoring them, I take to the bank and thrust back on my boots and tie the laces. The place where we laid Hull to rest isn't far but I can't go there now. I steer myself homeward. Home shouldn't fill me with dread. Home should lift my heart and hold it high. My home is hell itself.

I ignore the twitching net-curtains of the neighbours and stride back up the lane. I'm determined to dress myself and make my way to the Violet Cottage, where I will stay with Jude, Violet and Jane and my Dr Brady forever more. Nothing will make me stay with the walls and the horror of my hell.

My stomach rumbles as I glance around to see what's mine and what's precious to me. Nothing is. I throw my sodden coat back on over my dry dress. My bicycle wheel is flat and I dare not take Bredagh's. There is nothing for it but for me to take to the road, like a gypsy. Snot reaches my mouth, and swiping it aside brings more from my nose. There's a dark car slowing down. I raise my hand to greet whoever is gawping at me. I'm a sorry sight and the grapevine will have it told that I am in 'a bad way'.

The bus wouldn't take me to Dr Brady's house even if I could face the stares from them all on the bus. I'm a source of wonder at the best of times. The road blurs before me as I remember a time long ago when I stumbled with no direction and my saviour found me and took me in. The day is fresh and dry with a greyness hunkering over everything. I stride painfully on. It's not far in the grand scheme of the world. But getting to my new life is taking longer than I would like. I am sore all over, hunched as I snot into my sleeves and waver on the road. I long for Jane's arms as I turn into the lovely new gateway that Violet had made, and follow the fancy path stones to their back door.

Thin, tiny but strong arms take me into them without a word. Jane's floured hands pat my back and she mutters, 'Molly pet, whatever is the matter? Did you walk all the way here? You're all damp and it is dry outside? Lord love you little'n, whatever is the matter?'

Violet comes into the kitchen and holds her hanky forward as Jane hugs me in a few more times. 'Let her speak,' Violet says, as I sob on.

'Bredagh or Michael? Which of them hurt you?' Jane asks, waiting on my reply after I blow my nose. There's a silence apart from my chest thumping and my heart racing. 'Molly, your hair? Why are you wet me darlin'? Talk to us now, please?'

I shake on at my head and cry into her shoulder. 'We know she can take a beating, so it's worse than that. And where's Hull?'

Jane says at Violet. 'Whatever happened has hurt her heart. Look how she clutches at it.'

I'm weak with it all. The tea and bread lies untouched, despite all of their trying to get to me eat and drink.

'The doctor will know what to do. I'll get him in here now.'

The squeal that leaves me shocks them both.

'Jude can't see her like this,' Violet says. 'I'll get Richard, he'll make this better, Molly, I promise. We'll make this all better. Wait until I get Dr Brady.'

Chapter 22

I open my eyes. The room is familiar and the pillow is soft. It is mine, yet it all belongs to Dr Brady and Violet. There's a picture of The Hay Wain, which I love. There's nothing here that's mine, though.

I slept. The doctor gave me something, 'to calm me'. I turn over and see his beard smiling at me and his weight sits on the bed. I don't want to see his pity. I turn my back to him.

'It's bad then?'

I nod.

'Who?'

'Vincent.'

Saying his name makes vomit rise in my throat.

'Your hair?'

His hand is touching me, I don't want anyone to touch me ever again. I move away.

'What happened?'

The question brings me back to when my body was hurting. To when those hands were on me, and the noise of him was grunting and there he was pushing and poking.

'Don't ask me.'

'I've seen this before. Did he take you against your will?'

'Don't ask me that or touch me. Please don't touch me.'

'My poor Molly. I promise you that there are good men in this world. Caring, loving men and you'll find one like Jane reads to you about. There are good times to come, my little precious one.'

I close my eyes, tired of the promising I listen to. My patience is gone, waiting on these better days. Nothing will ever be clean or right again. No wishing, no healing, or praying will take me away from this knot in my gut and the scar across my soul.

'Did he hack at your hair?'

His tone makes it seem like this is the worst bit. I shake the red curls that are left.

'Violet's getting the tin bath out for you in the kitchen. Once it gets dark, take your time and wash it all away. We'll tell…'

'No-one.'

He's sitting on and the shadows are too. His air is sad, then angry, then sad again. Like them all downstairs, he's trying to fix me, make it all ease, but they weren't there when I needed them. I'm not going to make it easy for them. The doctor can't give me a pill or an injection to take all of this away. He shouldn't have left me there. I should have been here in this bed, in this home – for years. They left me to the demons and the walls that seep out badness. I was abandoned.

'Hull?' he asks me.

'Dead,' I tell him. I don't cry. I want to scream and roar but instead my limbs and stomach curl inwards.

I can feel his movements and him muttering, 'Mother of God.'

'Poisoned.'

He's crying; for his own honour which is ruined. He failed to protect us from the evil in the world. He has no right to cry, no right to be upset. Nothing has happened to him at all! All his life, he's been sheltered, protected and loved. He's lived with goodness in his walls and in those around him. He's never had to heal himself or had any reason to feel lost inside. The very sight of him does my heart good but right now I can't bear to near him.

'Please, go away.'

***

When I waken, I'm alone with the ceiling and the room. The bed is cosy and the air is warm. All is well in my brain, until I move. Then it floods back in, all of it washes over me and I die all over again. The night goes on. I start to hum. I hold my heart and between my legs. I urge the badness out and let the light of the morning in.

I take the large saucepan of boiling water off the range and toss it into the tin bath and place on another to boil. The soap stings my eyes but I wash and scrub until I am red raw. The water's milky and shallow but on and on I rub. I'm clean, dry and dressed, when Jane lifts the latch on the back door and comes into the house.

Jane's small but her smiles can fill a room. She takes off her coat. 'Let's pretend all is well with the world, eh?' Jane moves the kettle onto the hot plate and gets the flour to start on the bread-making she does. Her apron is wrapped around her and she looks at me between her chores. I sip lukewarm tea.

'The doctor says there's no Hull?'

She misses him too; his nose in her apron looking to be fed all the time, his paws muddying her floors, the dribbling water from his drink bowl by the scullery door. I don't want to think of never feeling his fur again, or hearing him bark.

'Them bastards,' she says.

I like her cursing. She chances it when out of ear-shot from the doctor and Violet. Jude copies her sometimes and she bribes him to stop with buns and cakes. Jane reads my mind and says, 'We'll just tell Jude that Hull died?'

I agree. Jude knows nothing of the badness in the world. I'm glad of that. It was decided a long time ago not to tell him of his blood or his relationship to me. He's never had to see Daddy or know he's not the doctor's and Violet's own son. No-one has spoiled his innocence – yet.

He's theirs and they're his. His life is better this way.

'You came here when you were eight. The age Jude is now. Times were hard for you then, Molly, but look how far you've come. How beautiful you've become and how strong. I know the doctor and Violet aren't fond of your healing, but don't let anyone destroy what you have. What Jude has. We must protect him now.'

I wish she'd stop that talk.

'Jude doesn't need to know of the past. His future is what's important.' She's afraid that I'll spill the apples of truth when my mind is in a mess. 'He's happy here and all is best this way.'

'Best? For who?'

She sits and looks at me. The tiles are earthen colours and have scratch marks and damage on them from the wear of time.

'It's best for Jude. Do you want him to have to deal with all you cope with?'

'I know to stay quiet.' I don't like my angels trying to get my attention now, either. None of it is good enough. Nothing they all do will help me. I wish they would all just go away and fuck off!

Chapter 23

'I'm not going back,' I announce on Sunday evening. The fire is lit and Jude's playing chess with the doctor. Violet is knitting. 'I'm not going back there in the morning. I aim to stay here, please, and pay my way.'

There's no noise from them and the fire leaps against the hearth. Sparks fly up the chimney as the log crackles.

'I suppose then that you aim to keep healing?' Violet asks clicking her needles together. Jude's eyes are wide and browner than any turf. His blonde hair comes from somewhere far back in time, as Mammy was dark and so was Daddy. There is no look of either of them about his features, but none of the doctor or Violet either. He may be tall, so they can claim him further, as both Richard and Violet are long and lean. Jude has a beautiful smile. He's almost pretty, like a girl, with rounded cheeks and jaw bones. 'You know that it isn't right for you to be at that healing?' Violet says when I don't answer her.

I stop my staring at the fire. Her own face is squinting and she looks harsher than she normally does. The doctor's on his feet with the metal poker in his fist. He stops in his tracks too.

'Richard, tell her.'

Dr Brady doesn't tell me anything, but goes to poke at the fire which is fine as it is.

'Tell her how it isn't right. You're a doctor and she's making a laughing stock of you… and it's not right.'

I lean forward in the soft chair towards her. 'I cured your bleeding.'

'That was just by chance. It was ready to stop. I was in such a low place then, I just thought it was something unusual. I jumped the gun. I shouldn't have been so quick to think it was… It was going to stop anyhow.'

The doctor coughs and pokes again at the fire, kneeling and keeping his back to us all. Jude's watching, his air curious and his mouth open. Knowing to be quiet seems to be a trait he and I share.

'I stopped your bleeding and you know it,' I tell her. Anger rises from the pit of me, and the shadows dance in their attempts to get me to be quiet now. I haven't listened to them for almost two days and I sure as hell am not going to start now.

'You have to see that you can't keep up the healing and stay here…'

My heart skips and leaps and my gut goes even heavier.

'I can't stop what is true to me.'

Violet snorts and her needles march on her lap.

'How else will I earn a living?' I ask.

'Like every other young woman. You'll do a decent day's work until you get a fine man to keep you and not be at that nonsense.'

The doctor's sitting in his high-backed chair now, a hand at his beard, pulling and scratching trying to make sense of the women in the room. She sounds just like my Mammy used to. It makes me want to vomit on their flowery carpet.

I don't want to give in that I may have lost my gifts anyway. When that animal humped me a big part of me died. I may never be able to touch another human being ever again. I may have lost all that is good inside me.

I can't believe, though, that Violet has lost faith in me as well. When did she start to think this way about the healing? I never discuss my work here any more. They ask me too much about it, but has Violet always thought I was a person that hurt them?

'The whole place tells the doctor that he's no good and you'll sort it for them. It has got to stop. Years of it now are taking their toll. They all talk about us being silly to take you in, when you're taking Richard's reputation and throwing it… in that river out there.'

Richard himself is in a bad way. His air is all messed up and hers is all tight. How did I not see this or feel this before? Where has all this venom come from?

'Violet, we said that we wouldn't harm her with all of this. Violet Cottage is her safe place. Molly is happiest here. We always said she would have a home here if she needed it. We agreed.'

'She can still be here but she must understand that to stay here – she can't be at that other nonsense. It isn't good for us.'

'Molly's gifted,' Jude tells them. 'She can't stop. Even I know that.'

'You know nothing of the world,' Violet's voice is raising higher. 'Our Molly knows how people are. She must understand that she is damaging Richard's reputation with her silliness.'

Richard's whole body is surrounded in a grey cloud, large and thick and full of annoyance.

'I can't go back there,' I tell them all. 'I can't go back to hell.'

Jude races over and throws his arms around me. 'Course you can stay, Molly. This is your home as much as it is mine. Let her stay, Mammy, please?'

There's never been this harshness in Violet before. She does find it hard to give full loving gestures to anyone but Jude. I get an odd kiss that lands on my cheek and the doctor can't get her to smile some days, but she always listens and responds to Jude with love in her heart. Always her air to me has been kind. Where has this side of her been hidden? It's a mystery to me.

'Richard, tell her what people are saying, especially this year. Tell her what you need her to do. Molly knows we care a great deal for her. Don't you, Molly?'

I'm not sure what I know any more. I can't fathom what's happening in the room, or outside it. I'm always unsure, uncertain of everyone, but here was always the same. I felt truth and justice lived between the people and the walls. Now it seems it is all a lie, or a dream.

'It's not as bad as she makes out,' Richard's lips say at me. 'But there's more talk of your abilities than mine. It's affecting our income.'

I know that income means money.

'That's it exactly,' Violet says. 'You need to know it. I don't want to hurt you, but you are harming us.'

'I think she's got more than enough to deal with, my dear. This is not fair. Stop it all now, please.'

Violet doesn't stop.

Chapter 24

Violet never was one to listen to the soft-spoken doctor. She knits on and says more and more about me being blind despite my gifts. 'You must know that it's all folklore and legend and that it can't be true really? You're playing with people's emotions and hopes. It isn't right to go on with it.'

'She's been hurt so much, Violet, be quiet now.'

Jude is at my side on the floor sitting listening to it all, cradling my leg in his young arms. 'What's happened to you, Molly? Who hurt you?' he asks up at me. Those brown eyes are full of goodness. 'I wish I could heal like you do. I think it is great, no matter what they say. Who hurt you?'

I pat his head like he was Hull and place a finger to my lips to silence his worries.

'If I can stay here, I will stop the healing,' I tell them.

Violet stops her knitting and reaches out her hand. It touches my arm. I feel the care I always sensed for her as her skin leaves the cloth of my blouse. 'Thank you, Molly. You're a great girl. We'll love having you here and we can think about a job for you as well. This is good news.'

'Will your Daddy let you stay though?' Richard asks me.

I ignore him and the worries which are attacking me at every angle. Daddy won't care much. I can picture Aunt Bredagh though, she'll miss her income. Violet is a formidable woman, but she's no match for a mad Aunt Bredagh.

My angels play with my hair and try to soothe me. I shrug them off me. Nothing will ever be the same, no matter what they do.

***

Aunt Bredagh bangs on the front door of Violet Cottage on the dot of nine o'clock. Jane's small body and worried freckled face comes flying into the kitchen to tell me even though I can hear Bredagh hollering for me to come out and face her.

Violet's standing her ground in the hall, despite knowing the doctor's gone out first thing and he's not in the surgery to the side of the house. Bredagh has lowered her tone, but I can still hear the words. 'I'm not sure what the likes of Molly has told you. She has some imagination. She needs to come out now and get to McLaughlin's. We've some people to see to there. You know yourself now, Mrs Brady. People don't like to be kept waiting.'

Bredagh has her hat and gloves on and her navy Sunday best skirt and jacket. There's a new scarf around her neck and she's got her face on; red rouge and lipstick. Seeing her in the nice surroundings, she almost looks as attractive as Mammy did. Thin and with an air of importance on her. I spy my coat on the hall stand and wonder how long it might hang there, with all of this going on.

'There you are! You rascal! Mrs Brady is telling me here that you aren't well? That you came here in a bad way? What's the matter with ya?'

Violet's mouth opens but it is Jane who comes out from behind me and stands so close to Bredagh that she has to actually take two steps back. She's nearer my coat on the hall stand. 'Our Molly's not well and you know why.'

In fairness to Bredagh, she seems genuinely uncertain as to why I am still in Violet Cottage and doesn't know what drove me here.

'Vincent had his way with me and I'm not going back,' I say to them all and my coat in the hall. 'I can't and won't heal any more. He's ruined all the goodness in me. If you want to be cross with someone – blame Vincent McCarthy!'

I turn on my heel to go back into the kitchen. I can hear Bredagh stumble out words to defend the animal and Jane saying, 'I know that violence like that could hinder the healing. I heard it somewhere long ago. Any sort of pain can disrupt the flow of such things.'

There's no talk of Vincent being an animal or a criminal. I stand around the corner and hear Bredagh, 'Watch your husband, Mrs Brady. From when she was no size that Molly McCarthy knows how to work men. I've seen her with my own two eyes. She can make men fall for her charms. I'll grant you, that it does help with the business we are at. They come back to ask for her hand in marriage and all sorts. I sometimes wonder, does she cast spells on them, or use her charms in other ways, if you catch my meaning. She may be one of my own, but I know that our Nancy, God rest her soul, had a hard time with her. Don't feel an obligation to keep her here. That's all I'm saying.'

Jane is straight to my defence. 'There's the best heart in her. I know there's none of that badness you speak of in her AT ALL and Mrs Brady here knows that too. Good day to you now!'

'Molly will be needing to come home. There's to be no more talk of her Uncle Vincent in that way too. Her daddy won't be pleased, if she's at that chat!'

'It's the first time we've heard her speak of such things,' Violet says. 'Richard feared as much, but as you say, she has him around her little finger.'

Jane must have the door open, as there's the smell of fresh air. 'Good day to you now... Molly's home is here now,' Jane says. 'Good day to you now.'

The door clicks closed and all is still in the hall.

'That one is one bad whore,' Jane says. 'How could you agree with her, about Molly?'

'It's easy for you to say such things. Molly's not staying under your roof and affecting your family. Richard's always had a soft spot for her, from when he came home and told me of this waif in that shack of a house and me knowing who he meant. Molly isn't all that easy to care for. If she's not going home, you won't have her day and night under your roof.'

Jane's whispering, 'I'll take her home with me if that's the issue, Mrs Brady, but you know she loves it here. This is where she feels most at home. How hurt would she be if she knew you said such things?'

'I don't mean any harm. I care a great deal for our Molly. But for years, she's made things difficult between Richard and I. Her healing has almost driven us under. She's only still a child herself. It's not fair on me to blame her for any of this. But we can't come between her and her family, either.'

'Taking Jude from his family didn't cause you to worry.'

It's then I hear the crack of a loud slap. I peer around the corner and see Jane holding her cheek.

'I think it is time for you to leave Violet Cottage. We can't afford you any more anyhow. I can't have you speak to me or my guests in the way that you have. You're getting too big for your boots. I'll pay you for the rest of the month, but please leave now.'

There's tears in Jane's eyes and her mouth hangs opens. Her eyes meet mine.

'Let's not bother Richard with all of this,' Violet adds. 'His health is already a worry. We'll tell him that we've come to an agreement and all is fine. Is that clear?'

I slink back behind the corner, as Jane makes her way down the hall towards me. Violet must be following her to go back into the drawing room as I can hear her say, 'I'm sorry, Jane. But until things improve we are not able to cover your wages any more anyhow.' The nastiness of Violet disappears into the drawing room.

I meet Jane in the hallway and wrap my arms around her neck. She kisses my cheek and we hold each other. Our bodies telling each other we will care and love each other until the end of everything. I leave her hold and take my coat from the hall stand. Without thinking, I open the door in a fluster and run out past the fancy gate posts and call after Bredagh, 'Wait for me. I'm coming with you.'

Chapter 25

Bredagh is all cocksure of herself as we walk towards Collooney. She is on her bicycle but hangs back to torment me.

'There's to be no more bad chat about Vincent. If he was to hear such things, he'd go mad, and who could blame him? He gives good money to your father and that would stop if he thought you were bad-mouthing him about the place. It doesn't pay to make the men-folk mad. You know that.'

The trees sway and the leaves rustle off them, falling at our feet. The fields are full of ripening corn that will be cut and threshed soon.

'He's gone then?' I ask her, as she peddles on, rabbiting about some of the people who'll be waiting on us at McLaughlin's.

'Vincent?'

'Yes.'

'I suppose he'll be away on the train by the time we're finished this evening.'

The village looks nice even though I'm on fire inside. The painted shop fronts and the cleaned cobbles are familiar and calming. Some of the people walking call 'hullo'. I know they mean to speak to me, as there's not much liking for Aunt Bredagh. 'Some of them bastards need a good slap,' she mutters as we pass the butcher's and one of the men whistles, 'Hullo, Molly darlin'.'

'That Jane O'Shea thought you'd not come with me. Did she not want you after all?' Bredagh sneers just as we reach McLaughlin's.

I walk past the line of people nodding and apologizing. 'Sorry we kept you waiting.' Bredagh props the bicycle by the door and we step inside.

'Don't answer me then,' Bredagh says pulling on my sleeve, 'but don't think of flitting off to them at every turn-around. That Brady woman sees through you, you know. She doesn't want a bit of ya. You're stuck here with me and don't be getting any more notions about changing the way things are.'

Something in me snaps. I grab Bredagh's chest. I pull her by her breast towards me and hold her firmly with my left hand and slap my right down hard onto the soft mound of flesh over her heart. 'I'll stop it beating,' I spit into her face. She manages to pull away from me but the shock of what I did is between us. I slowly take off my coat. 'Don't annoy me again,' I tell her as I lay my coat on the chair near the door. 'Don't annoy me again. I can stop your heart... like I stopped Mammy's.'

She's pale as pale can be when I look at her. 'Killed? You killed our Nancy?' she whispers. 'You couldn't... you didn't? I always thought...'

'Let's start on the people outside.' I pull open the back door to let in the first customer of the day. There's not a peep from Bredagh. Her eyes poke into me when she comes in with the teapot. She's knocked back a few whiskeys as the whiff of her is high and the colour is back to her cheeks. The harshness of her fills the room anytime she comes in and I fail in my healing quite a few times.

'I'm sorry I can't heal you today,' I tell some of them. Other times I stay silent and pretend I can do it. I wonder am I fooling anyone? There's too much pain in my own hands, too much confusion in my brain and hardness in my heart. In the finish I'm glad when the last person couldn't wait on me and leaves.

Daddy is usually perched on his stool at the bar or is hidden in the snug with Bredagh when I'm finished for the day, but neither of them are there. The corridor to the backroom is dark, but I step in the middle of each worn, orange tile, missing the cracks for fun, trying to lift the mood of me a little but it doesn't work and I stop my folly. My shadows are annoying me but I can't listen to them. I've left the door open and I see my coat on the chair ready for me to leave for the day. I can't wait to get into the fresh air.

Suddenly, things are not good. Vincent is in the corridor. Where did he come from? He stands there waiting on me to go through the door ahead of him. I freeze to the spot and a bad tingle goes down my spine. He winks and pulls me towards him. He stinks. There's grime on the collar of his shirt. I clasp my eyes shut when he licks my cheek. He nibbles on my earlobe and whispers, 'I missed you.'

He shoves us both on the few steps into the backroom and closes the door with his foot. The thud of the door closing brings a sweat to my forehead and back. 'There's no dog or anyone to protect you now,' he says, opening the top button of my blouse with both hands. I let him. I cannot move. Something makes my hand move to lean up on his jacket pocket, over where his heart is. He has my blouse open fully and whistles at my chest. He isn't noticing that my lips are moving and that his blood is slowing down. He grips my chin and it's then he feels weaker.

'Fuck,' he says and shakes his head a bit and stands back and away from my hand. The dread in me finds an empty bottle of porter on the windowsill. I grab it and smash it against the wall. The force of it cuts my hand but I hold the neck of the bottle with everything I have and slash at his face and neck. The bottle hits its mark before I even realise what I've done. I stab forward and stick it into his pocket but it doesn't go far in at all.

The bottle slips in my grip and clinks to the floor. I'm without my weapon as his blood pours through the moving fingers trying to hold his face in place. He's screaming now, roaring in pain. I've his blood on my skin and I'm trying to wipe it off me. Crying, I find the handle of the back door and am out into the darkness with people's voices behind me. I can't take much more of anything. I slump to the damp ground and rock over and back singing to myself and asking the Lord to make me die.

'She's cut me! That mad bitch cut me!' Vincent roars. 'Undressed herself and threw herself at me. When I refused, she cut me up!'

The murmuring of how to deal with me starts. It's then I hear Daddy, 'She'll not hurt me. She's my girl.'

Bredagh is breathless. 'I'm telling you, Michael. She said to me that she'd stop my heart, like she stopped Nancy's! Keep her away from your heart.'

'She held me chest and I felt weak as water. That's how she cut me. I didn't see it coming. She held me heart. That one is as evil as they come. Can someone get me the doctor?'

I hum on and on and let the darkness fold me into it. I want to die. Could I make my own heart stop? Before I can do anything at all, they've my hands held behind me and I'm being marched to a locked room with lots of anger following me.

Chapter 26

Daddy's eyes are bloodshot and swollen. I haven't seen him in a fortnight or more. 'The laundries are all full. Or so they say. They tell me that you must be punished but they can't keep you locked up here for much longer. The nuns said that they're scared of you. Sweet Christ, how have we come to this?' he says.

There is no word of Vincent being punished. 'I'm going to have a baby,' I tell him. 'I know that there will be a boy in my belly.'

Daddy cries into his hands. I wish he would just go away. 'Who...?' he asks like he cares.

'Vincent,' I tell him. 'He's a bad man and you know it.'

'Jesus! You can't say that.'

'I am saying it.'

'But...'

There's a knock at the door. One of the nice men in uniform steps in and says, 'Prison is the next stop, Michael. The nuns have refused point blank to take her. It's the Dublin women's prison. She's sentenced to time and that's it. I think we can sway the judge to be more lenient. She's been good in here for us. Not a bit of bother with her. We all have a soft spot for her. Don't we, Molly love? We all want to help.'

'Prison?' Daddy says and cries some more, making a holy-show of us both. There are no shadows or friends in the corner of my eyes any more. I've told them to 'fuck off' so many times, and they've listened now. The guards, too, have been sorry to hear that I'm not healing anyone.

'Michael, you do know that your Vincent is up to no good. You should know that he's well known for violence in the capital.

This is not your little one's fault. He has had this coming in a long while. We did our best for Molly, but the judge saw Vincent's face and listened to his lies and nonsense. Typical. And you didn't show up for her. An earning man's word is taken over a young girl's every time.'

'Is there nothing we can do?' Daddy asks him as they both make out I'm not there. 'That Dr Brady could put in a good word for her?'

'He already has done his best. The poor man is here often and spoke up, but sure we can't let him in to see her. She's considered a danger to herself and others. Even you shouldn't be here alone, but we gave you a few minutes' grace. The prison won't be pleasant, but it shouldn't be for too long.'

I'm not sure where I am, as I don't care to ask. It is possibly Sligo town from the noise of cars passing. The walls are cold and hard here in the lock-up. Although they don't seep badness out of them, they still don't let goodness in.

I'm glad to feel the wind in my hair as they stuff me into the back of a car. I'm as sick as a dog into the smelly bucket they give me. By the time we are inside the high walls of the Dublin prison, the men in the front seat are as tired of me as I am of life itself.

With the baby growing inside me, I cannot make my own heart stop. If I do, I'll kill the baby. This baby is important. I know in my heart that he's a special soul. Daddy mustn't have told anyone my secret cause no-one mentions it when I'm naked and they're checking me for lice. There's not a word of my baby when they are writing down all my information and slapping me on the back of the head to answer them, when they know it all already. When I'm still sick and need another bucket, no-one asks why or how they can help.

The board for a mattress is hard and the blanket scratchy. Despite the thick walls and the ice-cold bars on the windows, I feel safe. The place is crowded and there's not much room at times, but I don't care. The other women all leave me be and if they don't, I hiss at them and tell them, 'I'll kill you in your sleep. I'll hold your heart and make it stop.'

I don't look anyone in the eye and keep my hair over my face as much as possible. I'm safely locked away from what has hurt me in this world. There's no Vincent and no Aunt Bredagh. That is good.

I know now, too, that Dr Brady cares for me still, even if Violet doesn't. The thought of Jude worrying about me is about all that hurts me now. Perhaps he doesn't know where I am or what has happened. He's still only a child and might not hear such sad tales. I pray that he's always loved by Violet and that she doesn't turn sour on him, like she did on me.

They make us work unravelling old rope, but it's not as bad as it could be. I'm fed and can sup water when I please. I've no Bredagh in my face when I take a breather. The guards mostly leave me alone. There's one or two with bad air around them but they're mostly afraid of me. They've been told that I'm a witch and with my belly getting bigger they give me a wide berth. No-one wants to be accused of anything.

'I've watched you for weeks. You never speak?' a woman asks me.

If I don't talk then why is she talking to me? I know, like the rest in here, she sees me as a simpleton. It suits me that they don't rate me as a threat, or someone to bother with. This woman's hair is a funny shade of brown at the roots and is white until the ends. I hear her explain that she used to dye it when she was free to. She's probably old enough to be my mammy, but it's hard to tell. The gaol makes us all look pale and drawn. There's no proper daylight to keep us young looking.

'I'm guilty of nothing,' she says, and I sense a Sligo accent despite her attempts at talking all posh. 'I took on the nuns, that's all. The nuns wanted to sell children to the Americans, too, and they made sure I was caught. No-one believes me when I tell them that those mother and baby homes are full of babies going missing. The priests took against me, too. There's no hope for an ambitious woman that the men want rid of. Don't annoy the power in the world. I've learnt that the hard way.'

I rub my belly and thank the angels that I was not taken in by the nuns. This woman is called Peggy Bowden. I've heard the others talk about her. She's well liked and feared and she's also the first to mention that I'm carrying a child.

'I'm a midwife,' she tells me when we are alone and she reaches out to touch me. I don't want anyone near me and I shrink back from her. 'Who's the father?' she asks.

There's no way I can think of the father of my baby, and despite the kindness in her features and the air around her being soft, I'll never speak of him again.

'It's probably more correct to say, that I *used* to be a midwife.' Peggy laughs and it's a nice sound. I'm not sure I've ever laughed before. I must have laughed sometime. But when?

Peggy goes on, 'I'm not a midwife any more. They've ruined all of that for me. I'm only a criminal now. Why are the rest of the women afraid of you? They say that you've got powers? What do they mean?'

I don't answer her.

'The silent ones, like you, make them nervous. The chatty ones, like me, annoy them.' Her laugh is loud and long. The guards don't poke us back to work but nod at her. 'They're not the worst blaggards. Those two there have a good heart on them. But there's also the ones who want to grope you if they catch you in a dark corner and unaware,' she points at the men who are smoking and ignoring us. 'None of them seem to bother you much. It's mad to think they let me off killing my husband but then locked me up for giving children a better life in America.'

I touch my stomach.

'They say you did something so bad that the nuns wouldn't keep you? And that the baby is the work of the divil himself?'

I smile, despite not being happy at all.

'Molly? Isn't that your name?'

'Yes.'

'You do have a voice, then?'

'Yes.'

'They say you're not the full shilling.' She points to her pretty enough but funny coloured head.

'Yes.'

'They say the same about me.'

'Yes.'

'Can you say anything else other than yes?'

'Yes.'

We both laugh at that. I wait and laugh again all by myself. I like the sound of it. I laugh again and again. It feels nice to do it. The haze that I've lived in since the animal humped me lifts a little. I reach out and touch Peggy who's looking at me all funny. The skin is warm on her arm. 'Thank you,' I mutter.

'You're welcome, little one. You definitely aren't meant to be in prison. When they know you're having a baby, they can't keep you in here.'

I shrug. 'I'm safe.'

Peggy looks around her. She's thinking that I'm fully daft in the head. She looks at one bad woman after the next. 'I thought I was hard to most things, but there are days I could piss myself in fear in here. What kind of a life did you have, if this is a safe place?'

My shoulders lift.

'A beautiful creature like you would be such a threat out there. An unusual being people are afraid of. I don't think you're as simple as you make out, though. Can we be friends, Molly?'

'Yes.'

We laugh again together. There's a tiny feather on her shoulder. The angels must be happy that we have found each other.

Chapter 27

I still ignore them, though. The angels I mean. They do come to me now and again. In stubbornness and annoyance, I won't listen to them. I haven't done or thought about my healing in months. The only link to my past is the future that is in my belly. I rub and sing to him all the time; making him big, strong and perfect.

The days get better in the gaol, as they move Peggy and me closer. I hold her in my arms when her dreams are bad. Poor Peggy's mind takes off on her in the dark and she needs me. She'd never admit to her weakness but that draws me to her all the more. In the daylight hours she keeps vigil over me, thinking she spares me from the other villains who surround us and from the guards who want a piece of us.

'There's a new chaplain. A fine looker he is,' Peggy tells me. 'Priest or no priest, he has a fine set of teeth and a handsome face.'

I've seen him. I know that he's a troubled man. He has no interest in my beauty, but comes to whisper in my ear, 'I need to talk to you.'

I agree even though I have no choice as to what happens in this place. Peggy is sure that he wants to hump me like an animal. All he wants is for me to listen to him. He takes me to a quiet room where only I can hear of his worries. There is no point in my trying to explain it to Peggy that this man's pain has found me. I don't want to think about my gift, or talk of it. I don't want to go backwards, but in listening to this young handsome man, I sense that the future wants me to give in to being myself. I am what I am. I've not lost the gifts that were given to me.

'The child? You're carrying a baby?' the chaplain's beautiful lips ask me. 'Tell me about yourself. Let's talk about you today.'

'NO.'

'I looked at your information. They said you attacked and maimed your uncle?'

The wall behind him is uneven and old, with dips and hollows in the stones. It is whitewashed maybe.

'Why was I drawn to you, Molly? Why do you listen to me? Why is it that when we pray together I feel healed?'

I wish he'd talk on about his own sins, which aren't really sins at all.

'I want to know more about you. Why do I trust you and want to be near you? Do you know why, Molly? Are you used to people needing you?'

'Yes.'

'Are your parents alive?'

'My mammy is dead. Daddy's lost to the drink.'

'Where will you go when you get out? Where's home?'

'I have no home.'

'The child?'

'I'll be rich.'

His chuckle isn't a cruel one. He pities me. 'The guards tell me that you're friends with Peggy Bowden? She's not the best woman to take up with, Molly. I know in here, though, that she's the best of a bad lot. Despite what my superiors think of her, they tell me that she's looked after you. Is she good to you? You seemed to have picked your company as best you could.'

'She picked me.'

'I see.'

'When is she getting out? I don't think either of you have long left of your sentence. I might be able to arrange it that you are let out together. Do you think that would be a good idea?'

'Yes.'

'I won't want to let you go. I feel safe when I'm with you.'

'I like it here.'

His lip trembles. 'How could you like this hell-hole?'

'This is not hell. It is home. I'm safe here.'

Chapter 28

Peggy is good at counting and she is looking forward to getting out. The thoughts of everything outside scares me. I don't want to leave my last meeting with the chaplain. Everything about it hurts my ears and head. I cover my head with my arms and cry.

'She's in need of your protection,' he says to Peggy by the opened front gate. 'I'll miss her healing hands.'

The snorting Peggy does after him and her poking my arm is annoying. 'He likes what you did for him! The dirty brute didn't even try to hide what he made you do for him.'

I won't take my hands off my ears and clench my eyes shut. Nothing she says will make me move my legs. In the finish, she simply kicks my leg and it crumples under me a bit and starts me walking. She leads me like a blind, deaf mute and tells me off every few steps. But give her her dues, she still keeps hold of me and shouts at me above the noise of the people and the cars.

'Keep walking, you mad woman. We're free, Molly lass. We're free as birds. What are you scared of? This is freedom, you silly lunatic!'

How can I tell her that I've never been to a city before? And that I want to go back to where Vincent can't find me? He lives in Dublin and that's where I am now. There are no big high walls to hide me, or make me invisible. Everyone knows everyone in Ireland. It won't take long for someone to tell him where I am. Aunt Bredagh will be missing her money from my work. She'll be searching for me too.

The likes of them would know when I was going to be let out. I'm out early thanks to the chaplain, but I might still be found. Every face that looks at me could be someone who knows me from Sligo. They might be a relation of a person I healed, who will tell Bredagh they saw me.

'He'll find me,' I tell Peggy over a cup of strong tea in a place that sells it.

'Who will find you?'

The tea is sweet like Jane O'Shea used to make me.

'Even I don't know your full name, Molly. Why are you so frightened?'

'I've never been to the city before.'

'Where are you from?'

I can tell from her accent where she is from, so surely she can tell too?

'You still don't trust me?' Peggy asks.

'I don't trust anyone.'

My shadows nod at me. I want to ask them if Peggy is a good soul, but I won't satisfy them. I can't let them back into my life. I'm in enough of a mess as it is, without having more voices in my head. I'm tired of being pulled this way and that.

'Why do your eyes go all funny?' she asks me. 'Do you get fits sometimes? Are you sick? There's fits people get. Do you get them?'

'No.'

'You look downwards and to the sides all the time, like there's someone or something there. Who are you afraid of?'

I wish she wouldn't ask me things.

'The baby's father? I take it that you are not married?' she asks.

'I'm not married.'

'Your family?'

'My father is a drunkard and my mother is dead.'

'That must be the most you've ever said to me. Why were you in prison?'

I touch my baby boy and tell him that he's loved even though he was made in hate.

'The father of your child has something to do with all of this? Is that who you're afraid of Molly?'

'Yes.'

'Men have a lot to answer for in this world. I won't let anyone hurt you. You hear me,' Peggy holds my hand and rubs it between her own. 'You are safe with Peggy Bowden. I promise.'

Chapter 29

'What did you work at before?' Peggy asks me as we are staying in a room of some nurse she knows. The woman who owns the house doesn't want a bit of us. She stared at my large belly. The baby has always moved a lot, but in recent days he's running out of room, and so are we. 'You're too young for working. That's the answer. You were still at school?'

I let her think that I'm younger than I am. She knows I can't read or write but then there's many at school who can't do either. I stay quiet.

'You're pretty and men like you. You know how to please them,' Peggy tells me. 'We'll be all right if we can get you a decent job, once the baby's born. My face and reputation is well known in Dublin. It will be difficult for me to be a legitimate businesswoman again, but we'll make some money and look after each other.'

She rambles on at me about finding a home for the baby. 'I did it all the time when I was a midwife in Ranelagh. We left the babies where they'd be seen, like Moses in the bullrushes. When they were found, the guards got me to home the child with a rich family. I got money for minding the mother, and then for finding a home for the child. I did get caught at it. But this time I could make sure that a man I know finds your baby and gets it a good home.'

I know from listening to her, though, that she has no idea where the children end up. I want my baby to have a mother like Violet is to Jude. I know that someday Jude will be with me and so will my baby. In time, when I make my money, I will take care of them both. In the meantime, I'll need to make sure that I know where they both are.

'No,' I tell Peggy over and over. 'He's mine and I'll look after him.'

I do know that it will be difficult. But my baby will not be left on a road for someone to find, of that I am certain. He may be a son of an animal, but he's my baby. He will love me and I will love him.

'Will his father pay for him to be cared for?' Peggy asks me.

'No.'

'Can your family not take him? Aunts or uncles? Even if they don't want you?'

'No.'

'I can't house children, Molly. I'm not allowed. They won't let us keep him. If we're to make a living we can't have a child with us.'

'I see.'

'I'm sorry. I was told, too, that I can't live with children. I might be able to find a family who we can pay to look after him?'

This raises my spirits. 'I'll know where he is and how he is?'

'Yes.'

'You agree? It'll cost at least fifty pounds a year to do this.'

'Yes.'

I think of all the cash Bredagh took in from my healing. I get a large kick from the baby. He is nudging me to think of my gifts again. For both of us to be safe again, I may have to give in to the shadows and try to find my healing and bring it back to life.

Chapter 30

'This one will be ours, if you agree,' Peggy says, bounding up the front steps to number 34 on Mountjoy Square. 'There are tenants below the road and the top fourth storey is not suitable, but the first and second are ours. It's clean enough and has space for the business.'

It takes me a time to get up the steps and look into the street. I'm not sure what business she means, but I've a nice feeling about the place. Children are swinging from the lamp posts and there is a green field with trees to the front and down to the right a little way. On down the street is a public house, and further still is a butcher's. On the very end, and facing us, is a greengrocer's and public house. The building itself, as I look upwards, is very tall and matches all the others in the row.

I am tired of us moving about the last few weeks. I stand in the hallway and look at the bare stairs. There's an echo as Peggy calls me to walk to the end of the downstairs hall. I pass one small room on the left and enter a large enough kitchen. She has the back door open and I can see a nice paved yard with a washing line. The back scullery is tiny but cool and the kitchen has a new looking enamel sink and wooden dresser and a good modern enough range for the cooking.

'Well?' she asks me, all hopeful. 'How do the walls make you feel? You mention about the walls in places... What about these walls?'

I amble towards the stairs and ask the house and my shadows to talk to me. These past few weeks, I've given in to the angels wanting to help me. I realise that to heal others and keep my baby safe, I'll need to heal myself.

There is a sink and tin bath in an upstairs room and there are four other rooms, all coming off a fair-sized landing. Peggy's shoes clip up the boards on the stairs and she asks again, 'Well? What do you think?'

'I like it.'

'It'll cost us a lot of money. We'll need girls to make us a good amount, but I've some lassies who might work for us.'

'What will they do?'

'They will be whores, Molly love. Do you know what whores are?'

I should know what they are. I've heard the word used often enough. When Vincent had hurt me, I'm almost sure that he used that word.

'I'm not sure what whores are,' I tell her.

'They will lie and fuck with men for money.'

This stops me from going back down the stairs. I turn to look up at Peggy.

'No-one will force them?'

Peggy rests her hand on my shoulder. 'That's a deal, Molly darlin'. Each woman will only do what she wants to do.'

'Good.'

'Did the baby's father force you?'

'Don't talk to me about that. I'm safe now.'

'You do like it here? It's on Mountjoy Square and us having been in Mountjoy Gaol it seems fittin'. Imagine that? Maybe it's a good omen for us, Molly? Maybe we're home?'

Chapter 31

There are other girls in the house these days, but I mostly ignore them. One of them is called Tess. She is better to me than most, but even she makes me retreat into myself and talk with my shadows. I don't need anyone. Time slips by on me and then the pains start. Long bursts of agony ripple across my tummy and there comes a terrible pressure down below. I've decided to call the baby after a Gaelic warrior from the legends I heard from Jane. He will be called Fionn. He will be my Fionn, the warrior with a wise heart.

A peace comes to me with each spasm. My gift just takes over and it doesn't take that long. Fionn just falls out of me. All of the love in the world cushions his slipping out onto the kitchen floor.

'What in the name o' God?' Peggy races in the back door because she spies me sitting in the middle of the kitchen. 'Did you not think to mention he was coming?'

My baby lets out a wail. 'Fionn will not take your nonsense, Peggy.'

'He's to be the stuff of legends then?'

'Yes.'

'He's big enough to take on giants!'

She's right. Fionn is healthy and perfect, with all his fingers and toes, a button nose and dark eyes like our Jude and a cry that would crack iron. Fionn clings to my breast and suckles almost immediately and there he stays. He sleeps nestled in. He is my breath, my life and my greatest gift.

'You can't keep him,' Peggy starts. 'Women need to be married. He's a bastard. He will always be a bastard. He needs a family.'

Ignoring her isn't easy when she starts at me. Peggy wishes I could keep him, I know she does. We all want to be together, but life won't allow this. I'm a criminal, a fallen woman in the eyes of everyone. I live in a whore-house and this is no place for a child. I've been hidden away, but the shadows tell me, too, that I'm right to be fearful for Fionn's safety here.

'If I'm found to be housing children, I could be put back inside. And he cries that fuckin' loud! You need to be able to go outside and if you're seen with him, he'll be taken from you. Women must be married. You understand this? I can't go back inside. Even if you did leave here, where could you go with a child? Where? Can you go home to where you're from?'

'No.'

'Let's talk about him going to that nice family that I've found in Cavan.'

I don't want to talk about any such thing.

After a few months the time comes when I have to give in to the worst truth. I can't be a mother to Fionn without having a father for him.

Peggy takes me on the bus all the way to this farmhouse way out of Dublin. It's a better place than I thought it would be and the woman's pleasant and big like a cow might be, if it had a face.

'Himself is in the fields and the children are at school. I've got four of my own and we've taken in one already but he's ready for school now too. There's plenty of love and room here for another. We'll have him praying in front of the Sacred Heart soon enough.'

The walls are full of life and the fields have space for little legs. I touch the thickness of the house and stare at the woman who's looking to take my Fionn. I whisper, 'I'll be back for him sooner than this one with me knows. The angels will protect him. He's surrounded in beings and they'll mind him. You care for him like he's your own, or all the fires of hell will burn this house and all who you love.'

Peggy's ears are all cocked to hear me but she doesn't ask what's said. The woman's pale, but smiles on.

'She's not the full shilling… sometimes,' Peggy explains. 'Whatever she says, she's just sore now at leaving her baby with ya. She's glad that he's here. Aren't you, Molly?'

'I'll be back for my Fionn when I'm rich,' I tell them both.

'I hope he'll be easy looked after?' the woman asks.

'He'll have the angels to look after him.'

'Our Molly does love to talk about the angels,' Peggy scoffs. 'But there's always some truth in her few words.'

'There's no father I take it? I don't want to be bothered with callers looking to see him.'

'I'll be back soon enough,' I say again.

'Fionn will be safe here and well looked after. There'll be no need for you to worry.' The large woman starts on about the way her others are reared with silver spoons in their mouths. Peggy hands over the cash and I place Fionn into her arms. I bless him and kiss his cheek, whispering all the strength into him that I can find. God love the woman. She looks up into my face and there are tears in her eyes. 'I'll do as you ask, have no fear. Fionn has a home here. He's safe and won't need you to worry now.'

Leaving and walking away up the country-lane, I can't look back. My heart is sore. My angels pacify me, telling me over and over, 'This is good. This is the best. She means what she says. Fionn is home, for now. He's safe here. Keep walking. This is right for him. Like Jude, Fionn is loved and in a good home.'

Peggy hands me chocolate. I look out the bus window. All shades of green fly by and she's talking to me all the way, reassuring me and patting my arm. 'Fionn didn't cry, and you're not crying. What a strong woman you are, Molly. I'm so proud of you.'

'I'll find him a father who'll marry me,' I say to her when we get off the bus in Dublin.

'That's probably not going to happen, pet. Men don't marry women like us and they definitely don't father children like Fionn. Would Fionn's father marry you?'

'Never!'

'Please don't pin your hopes on any other men, Molly. Do you know any good man in this world?'

Dr Brady's bearded face come to my mind. If I wasn't so afraid of Vincent, Aunt Bredagh and Violet, the doctor might have taken Fionn as his own and even I might have been able to have a home. Jane O'Shea would help me find a man to love us both and I could be happy and safe. If only I could leave number 34 Mountjoy Square, too, without feeling like the world would harm me. With Fionn safe, I try to go every morning to Mass and then sit on in the dark chapel. I like being alone.

There's been talk in number 34 of me taking on to lie with men. My skin itches at the very thought of it. The house is so full of noise, gossip and nonsense that I like to sit in the silence somewhere safe. It's not far, but the routine lets me practice being alone for longer times on the streets. I've stopped looking at every face that I meet. The shadows have told me not everyone is from Sligo and not everyone is going to 'tell tales' to Aunt Bredagh. I still walk quickly with my eyes down and grunt an odd, 'hullo'. But I'm freer and content these days in the open. My hands burn with the healing and sometimes I wave them around in the chapel and pray that those near me find some goodness from them.

'Why do you hold your hands up like that?' a man's voice asks me. His hair's slicked back and he's very thin and horrid looking. The halo around him is as bad as bad can be. Being near him makes me panic. He knows Vincent, too, I can feel that off him. 'Where are you from, beautiful?' he whispers and follows me to the chapel door as the Mass is over. 'I've been watching you. I know most people about here. What's your name?'

'Leave me alone.' I scuttle off down the street like a frightened cat, but I know he's not far behind me.

Peggy's words ring in my ears, 'Do you know any good man in the world?'

This man definitely is not a good one. I'm certain of that.

Chapter 32

The other lassies in the house complain all the time. They are never done moaning.

'She doesn't take any of the callers. Why should she get away with being fed and watered? Other than cook, does she do anything? Her baby is gone now. She should work like the rest of us.'

Peggy doesn't pay much heed. But, I know by her that she's waiting for me to offer to earn something. There is no way I'm going to whore, if I can at all, but there's little else I can do. With no reading or writing, a fear of the city, and people, too, sometimes, I am a burden. Peggy raises the money for Fionn and I am grateful to her but not sure how to say it. The others' jealousy sits in the silences around the kitchen table, so, I set off to find myself another safer chapel to sit in.

After a few more daily sessions of listening to, 'she's a lazy mare', there's a knock to the door. With no-one else to answer it, the knocking comes again. I know if it disturbs the others, all hell will break loose. I go to open the large front door.

'I'm looking for Peggy,' the man says. He's blonde, young and has kind blue eyes. He's shifting himself from one working-boot to the other. 'They say there's women here?'

'Yes.' I look into his face and feel no fear at all.

'I need a good woman.' He's as handsome a young fella as I've ever seen. I like the air off him.

'Do you want to fuck with one?'

He blushes right out to his ears. 'I suppose I do,' he whispers, looking around behind him in case he's overheard. 'Me da says I need a good woman and to come here and ask for one.'

I close the door when he stands in the hall looking around him and up the stairs.

'Open your trousers,' I tell him.

His face is almost purple under the blonde hair.

'The others always check their men before they get any further.'

'What do you check for?' he chuckles. 'I have a cock.'

'Lice. Other critters.'

'Christ!'

I fold my arms the way I've seen Tess do. She usually puts on her thick spectacles to be sure when she's looking.

'Is it yourself that will...?' he stammers. 'I mean you're a beauty but before anything else happens, I'm wonderin' if I've enough money?'

'Maybe this time I'll just listen to you and hold your hand?'

His eyes widen and he watches me take to the stairs. His big heart is like mine. He's under pressure to do something he doesn't want to do. 'Your da sent you?' I ask when he follows me.

'Says it's time I knew what a cock is for.'

'The girls here tell me the same.'

He sits on my bed. I sit next to him.

'Your hair. Can I touch it?' He runs his fingers through the ends of it anyhow. I'm pleased that I don't mind him touching me. He examines a curl and says, 'Let's just talk then.'

Like the chaplain, he starts talking. I watch his stubbled jaw move and his full red lips open and close. His nose gets a rub with one hand as he takes hold of one of mine with the other. He lies back on the bed at a stage and he talks on about his life. At some point I lean back on his chest and he tells me that his mother is 'a wagon' and his father is harsh with him about working. 'I dream of escaping to America to become rich,' he says. His strong fingers play with my hair. I drift off to sleep listening to the sound of his voice. I waken when a door bangs downstairs and sit up with a jolt.

He's awake and looking down at me. 'You're no harlot,' he tells me and the niceness of him reminds me of Dr Brady. 'Can I come back to see you?'

'Of course.'

His boots move on the floorboards. I want him to lie back down. He pulls some notes from his back pocket and leaves them on the bed. 'What's your name? I'll ask for you again.'

'Molly.'

'What's yours?'

'Tommy.'

'Goodbye, Tommy.'

'You're a nice lass, Molly.' He touches one of my curls that's lying on my chest. 'A fine lass.'

'Goodbye,' he says and twists the door-knob. His feet on the stairs clump until there's no more of him.

Chapter 33

'The doctor is here,' Tess calls up the hall. I'm the only one in the kitchen. Peggy is at the shop at the end of the street. My heart does leap every time they mention a doctor. I always hope they mean my Dr Brady. But no. It's the man in his fifties, going bald like Daddy and wearing spectacles. He looks nothing like my Dr Brady.

'Molly isn't it?' he asks me when I peer up the hall. 'I'm leaving the package for the girls. And I have to tell Peggy that she may have some clients for her medicines room soon.'

'Thank you,' I tell him as we meet in the hallway. I take the wrapped brown paper parcel from him. His hand is soft as it touches off mine and I sense that he's very lonely. 'Maybe sometime we could... go upstairs?' he asks me. The thought of it doesn't make me want to vomit. He is a decent man, even if he does come here. His wife died and he misses her. We all know that. He is clean and well dressed and kind and has been with some of the others. I've heard them talk about him. They all like him and sometimes fight over him. I wouldn't do that, but he doesn't make my skin itch. 'You do know that you're my favourite girl here?'

I gawp at him. His small teeth are nice in the sunlight from the kitchen as I stand more to his right. The hall is narrow and his sleeve brushes off my breast.

'You don't talk much?' he asks. 'Is there anything I can help you with? My job is to heal?'

I chuckle.

'What's so funny? A doctor is a man of great power, you know.'

'Your knees hurt,' I tell him.

It's his turn to gawp at me. 'Yes.'

'Let me hold them.' I take his hand and lead him into the kitchen. He sits on the hard chair. I kneel in front of him. Muttering my prayers, I hold his knee-cap into the palm of one hand and wrap my fingers around the joint so that my fingertips dig into his muscle. He winces. The heat from my hands is hotter than it's been in a long while. I have to let go. He sighs. I do the same with the other leg and then take both together. When the heat gets too much I hover my hands over his hurt and soothe it away. His eyes are closed with his head tilted back and his mouth slightly open. 'They should feel better, I'll do more next time you are here.'

His eyes open and he rubs at his knees. 'They feel much better. Thank you. What did you do?'

'I'm a healer too.'

He's on his flat feet in his nice shoes and pulling at his suit's trouser legs in disbelief that he's no longer in pain. 'My goodness,' he mutters and we stroll up the hall. He stops at Peggy's medicines room door. 'Do you help the women who come here too?' He's checking to see do I understand what Peggy does in the medicines room.

'I don't help them. They come for Peggy. Not me.'

'She makes a lot of money in there.'

'Yes. She's a different kind of healer.'

'Some might call her a murderer. But the women I send to her are in a lot of anguish about their condition. They might need your hands on them?'

I take his wrist and there's a steady rhythm. His mouth opens and closes. My lips go towards his cheek and then his ear. 'After they lose the life inside them, it's all too horrid for them. I couldn't heal them then and they don't come back.'

His cheek is next to mine when he asks, 'They're afraid. Peggy warns them not to return here for all our sakes. Do you think it is a mortal sin what happens in that room?'

I kiss his cheek. 'Being forced against your will to do anything is not right. No woman is forced to do anything here.'

'You're right.' He nods and pats my hand that's on his wrist.

'You're a good man with a fine heart,' I tell him. 'Doctors must always be good men.'

'You're definitely my favourite. What a wonderful woman you are.'

'I will be a great woman someday.'

He leans on the front door when I open it. 'Take care of yourself, Molly. I'll pay to see you the next time.'

'What I do for you is our little secret,' I say. Over his shoulder, I notice there's a big black car parked opposite 34. There's a large man driving it, looking at me. 'It is our secret?' I ask the doctor.

'Yes. Peggy might be jealous if she knew you were someone who could help others too.' He's off down the steps and I notice that the car's gone. 'Goodbye,' the doctor says back to me and touches the side of his nose to tell me he's willing to keep my healing just between us.

He is right, Peggy would be jealous. Peggy is a damaged woman. Now that I am coming back to myself, I'm noticing things about her. She can be selfish, stubborn and vicious to others. I've always wanted a mother to look at me with love in her heart. Peggy does this for me every day and because of this, I will overlook almost everything else.

I love the goodness in Peggy, but even I see that it is slowly slipping away from us both.

Chapter 34

Peggy writes the address on the envelope every month to send the money to Cavan. We place it inside a card and I ask her to write little messages from me to Fionn. She does and always kisses my curls and holds my head in her arms afterwards. She longs for a child of her own. She has given up all hope of that happening. As she writes on the paper now, I touch her belly and hold my hand there. She lets me. I ask the stars to bring her a child.

'Tess got us bacon and cabbage for this evening,' she tells me as she moves away towards the sink. Her hands rest on the edge of it and she looks out into the backyard. 'Life is about surviving as best we can, but we must also try to make things better.'

'Yes.'

'We must dream, Molly, but not dream too big.'

'I'm going to be a great woman. I'll be rich someday and get Fionn.'

Peggy sighs.

'You must help me, Peggy.'

'Did you look around you lately?'

'You must not force me to...'

'I love you like my own.'

'I know.'

Tess strides in through the door complaining as usual about her lot and how we're sitting doing nothing. She doesn't like Peggy being soft on me. None of them do. Tess is on about some soldier who she saw on the way back from getting her cigarettes.

'Where were you?' she howls at me. I can't and won't tell her that I was at the best chapel I've found yet. One that's huge and smells of incense and echoes with the songs of angels even when there's no-one else there or any music playing. 'The soldier boy said he was seen to. He kisses ya down below and he is the nicest man to come about here. Someone seen to him? It must've been you?'

I'm away in my own mind. I am back at the chapel and listening to the lovely sounds. Tess can't break in, if I'm away there in my mind.

'I won't listen to this any more,' Peggy says. I'm glad she's stopped the annoyance. Tess keeps on at it, going on and on about how I'm everyone's favourite. She's probably meaning the bank clerk who keeps paying me to jump up and down on the bed and scream and laugh with him. He says he needs to have a 'reputation for the women'. I'm not sure what he means exactly, but he and I have such fun together. He pays me well and now and again he asks me to see my breasts and that's it. He says they don't do anything for him but I don't really care. He paid me more money to talk about him loudly outside the window of the bank. He was very generous for just two sentences. He makes up for the bastard who stole the money the doctor's been giving me for his knee healing. I don't know who took it. Peggy thinks I showed it to Tommy or someone else, but I didn't.

I know in my guts that Tess is the thief, but I can't prove it. She is a bad egg I don't want to crack. She'd ooze out a horrid smell, so she would.

Tommy is at the door again. This makes Tess as mad as Aunt Bredagh used to get. He never goes with any of the others and most men now don't seem to want Tess at all. Her teeth do make her mouth smell. She isn't the best looking with her greasy hair and bad temper. If I was a man, I wouldn't pay to put my mickey in her.

Tommy's arms are around me as soon as he is in my bedroom door. 'Can I stay overnight?' he asks as he takes off his trousers. 'Peggy will say yes. She'll let me stay, if you ask her again.' He loves being in my bed these last few times he's here and he's managed to get me to lie and sleep next to him.

His breath is nice in my hair and his arms are strong. In them, I feel safe. He's tried to get his tongue into my mouth, but I'm not ready for that slopping yet.

'I'm happy to wait,' he told me last time and since then I've thought about nothing else. What it might feel like to have his tongue in my mouth and his bare chest against me? I even wondered what his mickey might look like. In the bed now that he's sleeping, I take a peek under the covers. There's a bulge in his underwear and his chest is bare. The hair on his legs are fair and he has lots of long, thick hairs under his arms too. His smell is nice. I notice he has one eye open. 'What are you doin'?'

'Lookin'.'

'Do you like what ya see?'

'I do.'

He lifts himself up onto on one elbow. His lips touch softly off mine. They're warm and soft. I like them. I start at the slopping nonsense I've heard the others on about. There's a nice throbbing starting in me, a breathless panting and a deep want. Yes. It is like a need. I want to have him wrapped around me. With my nightdress off me in a flash, he is inside me before I really remember anything of Vincent. Suddenly my legs clench and my inside place doesn't want him in there. He's on top of my chest and I can't breathe. It's not his weight, it's the memories. He stops and holds my jaw and makes me look into his blue eyes. 'I love you, Molly. I'll never hurt you. Trust me.' I breathe out and try to let the worry away with it. He is not on top of me for long. He thanks me for the pleasure he moans into my ear. Then he snores. I take a peek under the cover at his mickey again. And yes, it is as ugly as I thought it would be.

Chapter 35

My latest chapel doesn't have any angel song in it today. The whole place is like an empty shell and the cold walls urge me out of the place. The walls there are normally fine and I don't have many other places to be. Definitely the chapel doesn't want me here today and my legs take me out the door and down the street. I get a whiff of cleanliness from myself as I move, and I like it. I've been getting into trouble for loving the bath and having longer time in it than the others. I adore the sound of water moving. I stop at the canal. It reminds me of the Owenmore River in Collooney. Near the canal brings some sounds I remember. The swish of the grass and the rustle of the trees, and Hull's bark. The fresh water on my toes brings me back.

Daddy took me once to see the sea. Only once. The wind was in my hair on that balmy day when we somehow got to the ocean. It wasn't hundreds of miles but the train didn't go to the ocean and so Daddy wasn't interested in it. The roar each time its mouth moved made it seem like a giant beast to me. 'Waves, they're called waves,' Daddy said. 'I can't stay here all day while you stare at them and play in the sand.'

'I love the sea,' I told him as he dragged me by the arm up the road with him. I waved at the waves until we went around a bend and they were gone. My ears still heard them until we turned another corner and then I cried. I knew it would be a long, long time until I'd see or hear it again. 'Do you love me at all?' I remember asking before I got a whack across the back of my legs from the stick he'd found in the ditch. The mark had stayed for days and burned when the raised blister had come off it.

Peggy's head pops out of the parlour when I come in the door of 34. There on the best chair is the bad man I met in the chapel a while back. I don't want to stay with the weasel, but Peggy beckons me in and closes the parlour door.

'This is a powerful man, Molly. He's called the Professor and he has noticed you at Mass. He has been trying to find you.'

Peggy is using her posh voice. I've heard Tess talk of this creature. She told us all that he is a man with many enemies. Like me, he can't read or write, or even count very well either, but he stole some papers from a university to make himself educated. He's got money all his life for killing and that's all he knows.

'The Professor wants to spend time with you,' Peggy says.

'All about here owe me money for… protection. No-one mentioned you girls.'

'We can come to some arrangement,' Peggy says, pointing at me. 'Molly could be yours for free once a fortnight… If you look after us?' Peggy purrs. I know she's frightened but I'm not her property. How dare she do this? I can't believe what I'm hearing. I cover my ears and hum.

'Once a week at least,' the thin man in the striped suit says. His silly hat is on the chair. I can picture Vincent in a similar one. My arms are itchy. I scratch them and search for my shadows.

'No,' Peggy says.

He jumps up and holds Peggy's face and says, 'No-one says no to me.'

'It is up to Molly.'

She needs me to agree. The air is thick like glue.

He doesn't realise how powerful I am. None of them do. The angels whisper that I'm going to be all right. They've a plan. I believe them. Peggy is urging me to agree to something to get him out the door. I can almost hear her heart thumping from here and can hear her words as they scream from her brain. *Get him out the door. Out the door.*

I look at this thin, short man from head to toe, like he's a piece of hen dung. I walk around him and the angels warn me that he's a bad animal and to be clever. 'Once a fortnight and I get presents,' I say. He sits next to me. It's then that I know that although he's a bad man, he can't do what Vincent did to me. His mickey doesn't work at all. It hasn't for years and this makes him angry and very dangerous.

'All the presents in the world for you, Molly. And if you're good, I'll pay you as well. Time is money after all.' He rubs his thin moustache down with his fingers and slicks back his hair. 'You gals will have no bother if people know that I come here.'

'That's good,' says Peggy.

I want to slap her smile all the way to fucking Cork.

He's grinning too, 'And sure there's no time like the present.'

'No,' Peggy says. 'Molly has a caller coming shortly. Not today.' Her wink is supposed to make me grateful to her. I can't look at them and start my humming instead.

The front door snaps him out onto the street and that is when Peggy changes to me. Like Violet – suddenly she is not mine any more. She is lost in a selfish haze and cannot or won't see how all this is for me. My talking with her stops. I hear her nightmares at night and I'm almost glad that she has them. Peggy's air is trying to change me too. I can't let it.

***

The clip of the Professor's shoes on the stairs is unmistakable. I can smell the stuff he lashes into his hair. Although his clothes are clean enough there are always stains of his food somewhere. The big man he has with him is called Tiny and he hides so much from everyone. The Professor trusts him but he shouldn't. The Professors knows sweet fuck all about anything. I decide what I will do, as his thin moustache comes around my opened bedroom door.

'Your father is angry with you,' I say from the bed and point to the chair for him to sit. My cardigan is buttoned to the top and he pokes at it as he passes me to sit on the chair. He notices that my skirt is long and my socks are pulled high. 'Your daddy's a grocer and is annoyed at you not taking up the trade.'

'Most of Dublin know that,' he says and pulls at his striped trouser legs, to rise them, to help him sit. 'Are you pretending to be a fortune teller or something?'

'I see things.'

'Pah!'

'I know you've marks on your back from where some men beat you a long time ago… over a horse.'

His beady eyes are wide and his hand motions for me to tell him more.

'You've marks on your ankle that won't come off.'

He pulls at his sock and shows me some ink marks.

'Half of Dublin could have told ya those things.'

'You have no children.'

'I do.'

'You don't. You have none of your own. You know you don't.'

He leans forward and points his thin finger covered in a thick gold ring into my face. 'I fuckin' do.'

'Your wife hates you.'

He laughs a bit at that. He doesn't care that she does.

'You're scared for most of the day. Tired and afraid every day. You sometimes cry into your pillow. You wish you could get away. Far away and live by the sea.'

He grunts, but is listening.

'You are like me.'

'Wha?'

'You want someone to love you.'

'Ha!'

'You're safe here with me. You can sleep here. I'll watch over you.'

'I aim to make a better use of our time. You stir things in me. Maybe…'

'That will never work. You know it won't. I see things.'

'You might change things for me.'

'I can try to heal what's wrong.'

'You're brave mentioning that to me.'

'I can help you.'

'I don't need…'

I place my finger to his thin lips.

'If you are good to me, I might try and help you. Otherwise, I won't.'

'You are some doll…'

'I know.'

He laughs again and smooths at his moustache. He is tired.

'Undress. Get in to bed. I'll sing to you,' I tell him.

'Maybe next time I will.'

He's gone. There is a noise of him on the stairs leaving and he's shouting to Tiny. I breathe again and thank my shadows.

Chapter 36

The waft of cigar smoke reaches under my bedroom door and my gut clenches. The Professor is back. I'm his whiskey. He says that he needs me more every time he sees me. I think he also needs the sleep. Most of the time I sing to him and he snores, or he gets me to tell him things about his past. He doesn't ask about his future. He must know in his own way that he'll die soon enough. I can't see exactly how it will happen, but he will be shot.

Peggy has big guilt at leaving me to him. She asks me all the time what he's like. She worries that he forces me to do things.

'Do you hate fucking him?' she asked me this morning. I should have put her mind to rest, but I didn't. For her own gain, she forced me into a cage with a lion. Her eyes don't hold the same care for me that they once did. Like Violet, I suddenly don't know her. She cares for me, but resents me too.

Yet, I've done nothing wrong. When men ask for me, she flinches. Sometimes she even rolls her eyes. Since Tommy and I have laid down together, I don't find some of the others too bad. None are like my Tommy, of course, but I only take the ones that aren't rotten inside. It seems, too, that the men talk and my gifts bring men lots of pleasure. It seems that I just know what to do. Like the healing, it comes naturally. I like the control I have over them and I admit now, that I enjoy that. In ways, it's another form of healing for me. If I don't think of it as 'sin', or if I am not reminded of Vincent, it's not so bad at all.

Without looking at the Professor, I can tell that he's the angriest he has ever been. He is not cross with me yet. The room is full with the spirits of men he has recently killed. I'm afraid as usual that I'll lose control of the air around him. He yanks off his belt and throws off his shoes. He is too wound up to sleep. I'm going to have to tread carefully, but he's not in the mood to listen either.

'How many are dead now, oh wise Molly? Tell me how many are dead because of me?'

'I have a son,' I tell him. Children might calm him. 'I want to visit him. Will you take me in your car?'

He flops onto the bed.

'A trip. I'd love to see the sea too,' I'm pretending that he is a normal man and that this is a reasonable thing to ask him.

There's a bed squeaking next door. This makes him more annoyed. 'FUCK, you ARE a halfwit! I come in here screaming about the men I've killed and you want to take me on the trip to the seaside with your child?'

'Wouldn't it be nice?'

'No.'

'I do lots for you.'

'You do?' His lips clench together. 'You are a whore, who doesn't do any whoring!'

'That's not my fault.'

I've poked the wrong cross dog. The belt in his hand lashes out. It misses me and hits the brass end of the bed. He swipes again with it as I scurry up onto the bed and into the corner. The leather reaches my back with a crack and then another. It stings like fuck. I even use that word.

I hear him say, 'I'm sorry.' He isn't sorry at all.

I'm so tired of people. I turn and point at him. 'I curse you. I call on the darkness to come for you.'

He slumps to the floor.

'You don't deserve my help. Fuck you!'

'Don't, Molly. Don't use those words. It's not like you.'

'I call on death for you now – for hurting me.'

He doesn't speak for a few moments and when he does it's a whisper, 'How will it happen? When? Let it be soon.'

'It will be when you least expect it.'

'Here?'

I get up off the bed and look down on him where he's sitting like a little boy on the floor. 'I won't let death take you when you are here with me. I'll keep you safe if you promise to never hurt me again.'

'Call off the curse?' he begs.

'If you promise to help me get my son back.'

'You have my word.'

His word is not worth much, but it is all that I have.

'I need a husband and a home.'

'I can't marry you. I have a wife.'

'To get away someone will have to marry me.'

He shrugs. 'Where is your son?'

'You'll help me if I need it?'

'Yes. But…'

'You'll help?'

'What are you thinking of? You're a mad woman.'

'You'll know when you'll be able to do something for me.'

'I will do all that I can, if you lift your curse? Sing to me,' he says as he hauls himself onto the bed and pulls off his shirt. 'Make me better.'

I don't have to sing for long. He nods off and I fall asleep sitting like an idiot on the chair. I don't hear him leaving until his shoes hit the stairs.

'All good?' Peggy asks him when I listen from the landing.

'Never better, Peggy. Never better.'

'Good.'

Peggy has been washing the floor, waiting on him. She says, 'I aim to move premises. Know of anywhere?'

'Why move, pretty lady?'

'I aim to get more girls. More quality customers like yourself. I also have a sideline business…'

'Sideline? You never said.'

'It's not worth mentioning. But if I got better premises?'

'That's right. You went inside for selling babies.'

'I didn't sell them… I helped…'

'Course you did.'

'I don't go near children any more.'

'What is this sideline business then?'

'I give women… relief from… being in the family way.'

'Fuck! You're a butcher?'

''Tis easy for the likes of you to laugh. Some women are desperate.'

'And you do them a good turn? A handsomely paid one?'

'There's hardly any coming these days. With me here and all… I'm not as respectable.'

'Respectable, eh? You want to go upmarket?'

'Yes.'

'You want to get the bastards out of rich bitches?'

'I used to be a midwife. I know my stuff. I like number 34, but I think I could be better. Make things better for myself and Molly.'

'Do you now? Molly mightn't want to go with you.'

'Molly is my family.'

'You whore out your family? You're some doll, eh?'

'Molly chooses…'

'Leave it with me. I'll see what I can do. I might find other ways we could do business. Whore like you with brains and ambition? Who knows what we could do together.'

The angels better tell me their plans soon. I'm starting to panic and I don't know why. Things might have to get worse before they get better. Why are things never good and easy for long?

Chapter 37

Tess takes to teasing me that everyone 'loves me best of all'. I know it used to be true about Peggy being softer on me than the rest. Peggy, though, is less fond of me when I'm a threat to her. Like Violet, when I was weak and helpless, she accepted me. When I started to get a power all of my own, this got in the way. Mammy resented me all her life and Aunt Bredagh too. The only true loves in my life are a dead dog, a man called Dr Brady and small Jane O'Shea.

'They all love Molly.'

'Shut up! That Professor doesn't love me,' I say to Tess. I can't eat my porridge.

Tess giggles on.

'He only loves himself, Molly darlin'…' Peggy says. She looks terrible. Her nightmares must be bad again.

'None of them want ta marry.' I'm trying to work out a plan. A time and a way to get out from under everyone's control. I need to be free as bird. Soar away, high into the sky, make my way over an ocean. I'll have to go on the waves and let them help me get far, far away from all of this mess.

'I'm not married… now,' Peggy adds.

'Cause no-one is asking ya.' I am being cruel. I want to hurt her. I can't help myself saying again, 'Cause you're old and no-one is asking ya.'

Tess really laughs and Peggy flings the dishcloth at her.

'One man did ask me once. Mick Moran was his name. God bless him. The other fecker wasn't a choice, I'll grant you that. But being married isn't all sunshine, Molly.'

'I wanta be married,' I tell her because it's true. Marriage is what all good women want and need. I'll need a father for Fionn and the babies I aim to have. It is normal for a woman to need and want a husband. Everyone should have someone to love them. Even me.

'They'll not want your Fionn,' Tess chirps in. 'Men only want their own children. Like lions, they don't want another lion's cubs. And Irish men want virgins.'

'Like Our Lady?' I say.

Tess laughs again and looks over at Peggy who says, 'Irish mothers want good girls for their sons. You'd want a nice quiet girl for Fionn.'

'I want Fionn for myself.'

'Exactly.' Tess shrugs and eats her porridge.

'If men think we're bad, why do they want us?' I poke Peggy to annoy her even more. 'Why do they tell me Molly is their favourite?'

Tess sighs. 'They want us. But don't want us.'

'The Professor says he needs me.'

'He needs you for a quick poke, Molly. He doesn't need you forever. He doesn't need to marry you,' Tess says.

'But… I'm good…'

'You are good, darling, yes. It's them that are bad. Christ, at this hour of the morning it's all very confusing.'

'All is bad.' The mug in my hand gets a clunk onto the table.

'Yes. All is shit.' Peggy has her hands in her hair.

'But you said you'd make it all better?'

Tess sneers. 'She lied to you. Nothing ever gets better.'

I get up off my chair in one movement. It topples over. Tess is right. Peggy lies to me a lot.

'I didn't lie, Tess,' Peggy starts but I'm out the door. I stand to eavesdrop in the hallway.

'It's desperate that we need her. They all want Molly,' Tess grunts. 'Professor, the soldier, the sailors. Jasus, if a candlestick maker arrived he'd want her too. The rest of us need a chance. None of them ask for me any more.'

I hear Tess wash her bowl.

'Did you get any letters recently?' Peggy asks her.

'Bitch,' Tess spits. 'Don't you take the post in most mornings off the floor? You know they don't want to know about me.'

'Jesus. Sorry for asking.'

'Sorry. Just I heard ya say to the Professor you're thinking of moving.'

'Course I'd take you, Tess,' Peggy lies. 'Sure, you are like the furniture.'

'Are you taking the old furniture? There's nothing much in this place.'

I wonder if Peggy had no use for me, would she bother to take me with her? It is then that my shadows remind me that I might not want to go with her. How will I escape? I wish they'd tell me. I'm getting tired of waiting.

Chapter 38

'They're fighting,' one of the girls shouts. 'Fuck's sake. Drunk they are. Do something, Peggy.'

A male voice shouts, 'She's got a gun.'

'If you don't shut up, I'll use it,' Peggy shouts, her blonde hair sticking out in all directions. She looks funny. 'There's to be no men here overnight. Shut the fuck up, or get out.'

I had been enjoying a bath, until Tess started telling tales on me. 'She was in the tub again, Peggy. Getting her boyo to carry up buckets of our hot water – them sitting on the warm plates on the range for the morning.'

Tommy is standing with a bucket and him in his jocks, looking like he's been caught stealing the sweets from daddy's tin on the mantlepiece.

'Get back to your beds the lot of ye,' Peggy hollers and cocks the rifle higher. 'There should be no men here at this time of night.'

I tug on Tommy's arm and we go back into my room.

'It isn't even loaded,' some fella says.

Peggy screams, and fires the gun. The noise rings in my ears and I find a feather sitting on the floor in my room. The angels tell me this is the start of things. The bullet lodged in the wall will start the events that will take me away and get me better days again.

In the morning, there's a garda, a man of the law, in number 34, asking about the shot and the rifle. Peggy is on edge. She's lying about where she got the rifle and there is talk of the Professor and my ears open wide.

'Professor bothering ya at all?' the sergeant asks.

'Who?'

'Arrah now, Peggy.'

'No. He's good to number 34.'

'Is he now?'

'Would you be jealous, sergeant?'

'Course not.' He pulls at his jacket and makes the buttons all stand in a neater row.

'If you could tell me anything, the law would be grateful.'

'I may be many things… but a snitch is not one of them. Now, I've work to be doing.'

''Tis me who should be cross, Peggy. Me, who helps keep things all quiet at the station for number 34. Don't be dragging attention here again, now. Do you hear me?'

Tess starts on at Peggy when the sergeant leaves, teasing her about him 'having a soft spot her'.

The day goes on and I take a trip to the chapel and the canal. When I come back, Tess is all delighted to tell me, 'Tommy was here. All wet. The Professor threw him in the canal and told him to stay away from you.'

My mind and heart is in a spin. If Tommy stops calling, I'll have no-one to help me get away. I'll definitely have no-one to marry me. What if Tommy stops coming and won't rescue me like I hope he will?

Chapter 39

'This Tommy fella. What's so special about him?' Peggy is asking. 'When we got out of "The Joy" he helped pull you out of the dark place you were in. He is soft, I suppose, and handsome, but is there more between you?'

'He makes me tingle.'

'Tingle?'

We are peeling spuds for the midday meal.

'He wants to marry me.'

I'm not lying as such. Tommy did ask me in a fit of sin one night. I hadn't answered him but Peggy doesn't need to know that. Peggy is worried. Like Aunt Bredagh, I'm part of her income and the Professor wants me here in number 34.

'Has he means to keep you? Does he work?' she asks.

I'm being cruel to her. I want her to worry.

'Did you meet his friends or family yet?' Her head bows low trying to get my attention at the sink. 'And Fionn? Does he want him?'

'Course.'

I never lie. I hate it more than anything. I've never once mentioned Fionn to Tommy. The angels told me not to bother. It hurts my stomach to think he wouldn't love me any more if he knew about my child. Tommy does love me, I know he does, but he'd care too much about the 'look' of things. He has an idea, too, about my healing as I rub his sore muscles some evenings. I told him a little about being able to see people's air. He thinks I'm touched, of course, and wants to protect me. He is a sweet fellow and no more than myself, he's controlled by his terrible parents.

'The Professor likes you,' Peggy says at me. What does she want me to do with him? I don't understand her. If she cares about me at all, why is she forcing me to be with him.

'He'll not marry me,' I tell her. He can't be my escape to happy days and love. He might be her way of getting out of here but he's not mine.

'He likes you and he's a dangerous man to make angry.'

I take the knives and forks from the drawer and the plates down from the dresser. Does she care about anyone other than herself? I want to stick a fork in her eye.

'Did you tell the Professor about this young fella?'

What does she take me for? A complete fool? Of course she does. Molly the halfwit, that's me.

'The Professor is jealous,' she says, taking me by the hand. 'Men get angry when they're jealous. People say he does terrible things to those who make him angry.'

I can't let her touch me. I pull my hand away and want her to know exactly what she's leaving me with. I unbutton my blouse and turn around.

'Did the Professor do this? Did he do this?'

She is blind like Daddy was. She doesn't want to see what's before her.

'What happened? What happened, darlin'?'

'He doesn't love me and did this.'

'Did you ask him about love? But you don't love him?'

'I might if he'd marry me and help me.'

'You won't ask him again?'

'No.'

'Good girl. You've got me. I'll always look after you.'

'You said you'd make things better.'

'But it takes time. Time to make enough to move us out of here. Molly, you cannot fall out of favour with the Professor or we're stuck and in trouble too.'

This all sounds far too familiar. My memories come flooding back. Daddy telling me to be good to him and Vincent. Mammy jealous of me and hating me for making her look bad, Daddy thumping me, Aunt Bredagh screaming, Vincent naked, Violet cross with me. I sing a bit to take me away. I need to get to the ocean.

'He is a powerful man,' Peggy says. 'If anyone can get us out of here to something better, it's the Professor. And you can make it happen.'

'He'll not marry me,' I tell her again.

'No. But he likes you. He got angry, that's all. He'll want you in a nicer place. Just leave the asking to me.'

'Fionn too. He'll let me get him too.'

'Yes.'

She is lying to me.

'Tess?' I ask knowing if we get out of here, she has no notion of keeping Tess around for long.

'And Tess. Of course I'd take Tess too. But let me do the talking. You don't want the Professor to hit you again. He was bad to hit you,' she whispers. 'It was wrong.'

'I won't see him again? You make it all better?' I need her to say she will look after me, protect me, care for me like she's promised. But no.

'If we're to get him to take us somewhere nice then you need to keep him sweet on you. And you need to get rid of that young fella, too, that keeps calling.'

Peggy has let me down yet again. 'No.'

'Okay, Molly... but the Professor might get rid of him if you don't.'

The Professor better not touch my Tommy. I couldn't bear it.

'Let me do the thinking and the talking,' Peggy says.

She reminds me of Aunt Bredagh. And I've always wanted to kill Aunt Bredagh!

Chapter 40

Tess is plaiting my hair. I don't really want her hands in my hair but she insisted. She's trying to be friendly because if we leave number 34, she will need a home with us.

'I hate what we do,' Tess says.

'I like doing it,' I admit. I never did think I'd like a man humping me, but I thrive on controlling them. I grow stronger with them panting and begging, and throwing money on the bed. It's not that bad at all but I do feel sorry for Tess if she doesn't want to do it.

'We know you like it. But you can't like it *all* the time?' Tess says. 'There's only a few that'll want to see you're all right. Most don't care. Like that soldier fella. He's a *lover*.'

I laugh at her. Tess holds my hair and pulls, 'Like you don't know, ya wagon. Stealing him from me.'

I didn't steal her soldier. But she stole from me!

'Don't lie. He said he was seen ta and he was askin' for you. Like all of them that are any good. They all want their favourite Molly.'

'You could be a hairdresser and you're a good cook,' Peggy tells Tess.

'I make more money at this. Quiet these days though, eh? Professor might be scaring them off. Or the sergeant calling.'

'Nothing we can do about either,' Peggy admits.

'Suppose not.'

'I'm gonna get Fionn soon,' I tell them to shut them up.

Tess throws her eyes to heaven. 'There's no talking to the likes of you.'

'I will make things better myself.'

'All by yourself?' Tess asks.

'Tired of waiting.'

'Aren't we all,' Tess replies. 'Fed up of fucking.'

'What are you going to do?' Peggy leans forward in her chair. 'The Professor won't be too happy if you flit off on him and I don't fancy dealing with him if that happens.'

'He isn't my problem.'

'Aren't you all cocksure?' Tess rolls her eyes. 'If he gets pissed off, he's all of our problem.'

'Think or talk to us before you do anything,' Peggy begs.

'My life.'

'The cheek! And Peggy hasn't been good to you or nothing?' Tess says.

I bite my nail to stop me from screaming at them both.

Peggy's voice goes all posh. 'I care about you, Molly. More than anyone. I worry about you. Look out for you.'

'You use me. You,' I point into her once pretty face, 'YOU, use me.'

Chapter 41

'I promised you a present,' the Professor says as Tiny carries in a big box and puts it on the kitchen table. This is going to drive the other girls wild. They never get presents. He has his arm around my waist pretending that we are like a man and woman should be. He smells of death. It wrinkles my nose.

'Do you not want to open it?' Peggy snaps.

I don't need to. It is a gramophone record player.

'It's an expensive gift. Say thank you, Molly,' Peggy says at me, when she's taken off the brown paper wrapping. I sup my tea and wink at the Professor. He knows that I love music.

'You're welcome, Mol. I'll do anything for my Molly.'

'For fuck's sake,' I hear from eavesdropping Tess outside the open door.

'Molly's a lucky girl,' Peggy says in her posh voice. I want to stab her with the scissors but, of course, my protectors won't let me. The good days are coming, if I just have patience.

It's May before I know it and the sunshine brings out the happiness in everyone. Peggy and the others are in the backyard watching the sheets batter about in the breeze. I love my records. I only have two. One is all the way from America, across the ocean. 'Summertime and the living is easy', and the other is 'Molly Malone' who had her barrows of cockles and mussels in Dublin.

I love to dance and sing. It lifts me up and away. My summer dress is stuck to me but I dance and sing on. 'Your daddy's rich and your mama's good-looking…' This always makes me smile. Daddy being rich? Ha!

Tommy is standing in the hallway when I dance out there. He is not looking good. There's a gash over his left eye and he has blood on his shirt. I take him to the sink in the kitchen not asking him anything.

'You know about this?' he asks. 'You know who did this to me?'

'I only know what I can see.'

'The Professor's big lad, clocked me one. I'm tired of ducking and diving because of you.'

'Me?'

'I won't have you with other men any more.'

'Then marry me,' I tell him plain as day.

'My da and ma wouldn't allow it.'

I've stopped his bleeding but I wonder should I start it again. He is on about them again. There is always an excuse.

'Are you a man at all?'

He gets up on those sturdy legs of his and tries to make me feel small. 'You're not someone they'd… You aren't stupid like everyone thinks. You know what I mean.'

I fold my arms and wait for him to go on.

'I mean, you don't… I mean…'

'Are you going to rescue me from the Professor and take me away or not?'

He paces and has his hands in his hair. 'I wish I could. I want to…'

'You want! Pah!'

'Don't, Molly. Don't be like that now.' He tries to hold me. 'I need ya, Molly.'

'But that is not enough.'

'I'd do anything for you.'

The sound of his lies is unbearable. He loves me, but is too scared of his own situation to do anything about it.

'You're a mouse of a man.'

He lets go of me. His face is red and his jaw tight. 'Stop that chat now.'

'You don't do anything for me. You are selfish like all the rest.'

'I take a beatin' for ya and this is the thanks I get!'

'It's not my fault you won't stop coming here.'

'Do you want me to stop? Everyone wants me to. The Professor, Tiny, my ma! Me da thinks that I'm a big eejit. And Peggy. They all want this over with.'

'I want this over one way or another!' I start washing the dishes in the sink to do anything rather than have to deal with him.

'You want rid of me?'

'You'll go like all the rest.'

'I can't believe you think that. I won't leave you. Don't make me,' Tommy says.

'You will leave me like all the rest.'

'Stop that.'

'I have a bastard son, Tommy.'

This stops him in his tracks. He is thinking of me with other men now. He sees his mother's disgusted face and his heart crawls at the thoughts of another man's child.

'No?' he breathes. 'Where?'

'I'll get him back and we can be a family.'

'NO!'

'Yes!'

Like lightning, his hand is in my hair. Tangled in amongst my curls. He promised to never hurt me but his grip is sore and he tugs me towards him. I'm back in under Vincent when Tommy shoves me and pins me against the sink. There's a knife I've washed at my fingertips. There are no voices telling me that it is Tommy, and that I love him, and to stop. Vincent is all that I think of and every inch of fear and loathing makes me fight out of his grip. The knife moves with me and slashes his side. He lungs at me and I stab, whack, slice whatever gets in the way. Years of pain are screamed out of me. There is blood. There's a lot of blood. I roar again and drop the knife. It was as quick as a blink – as fast as that.

I fought back.

My hand trembles and there are women screaming. I'm in under the table and Daddy has just thumped me, the chair legs shield me from him. He laughs and tells me that I'll have to be grateful and do what I'm told. Peggy is saying similar things. Giving out to me. Then trying to get me to come out.

'Molly, what's happened? Where is he?' she is asking.

'Gone.'

Tommy is gone like everyone else is.

'Is it you that's bleedin'?' Peggy asks.

'No.'

'You sure?'

'Stabbed him.'

She kneels to look in under the table. 'Where is he now?'

I push my hair out of the way. All that I know is I am going to get away from them all. I might even get back to prison now. That wouldn't be so bad, but they won't let me have Fionn there.

'Come out of there. Let me see you. I'm worried.' Peggy pulls at my arm. I thump her hand off my arm. 'Is he definitely away?' she asks.

'Yes. Gone. Won't marry me. Doesn't want Fionn.' I hold my knees to my chin and close my eyes. I'm by the sea and all is grand. My Dr Brady is with me and Jude too. Fionn is in my arms.

'Who needs a man, Molly? Sure, you have me and the girls. Please come out. Tell me what happened. Please? Molly.'

I can't be here. I have to be away somewhere else.

Peggy is getting cross. 'I'm going to have to clear up this mess. You silly girl.'

'Do ya think she killed him?' Tess asks.

'Wouldn't think so or someone would be calling.'

'She needs to be taken away.'

'You'll go before she does,' Peggy says. 'Talk to me, Molly.'

The kettle whistles into a boil.

'We'll be all right. Just you wait and see. We could put on some of your music? Do you think you hurt him bad? Did you hurt men before? You cannot do that again. Do you hear me? You cannot use a knife like that. They'll take you away. Take you from me.'

I fix my hair and stand looking out into the fading sunshine. Going away is what I need. The anger in me rises again, I can't stop it and there are no angels. Whatever is in their plan is happening. Why does everything have to be so hard?

'I need you here,' Peggy says. 'I need you to stay with me. I need you with me, Molly.'

The cheek! I laugh at her. I like the sound of my laugh. It rises high and all around us. I spit when I say, 'I don't need to stay with you. I hate you.'

Chapter 42

The truth is, I don't hate Peggy. Much as I try, I can't even dislike her much. I just know that the time has come for me to leave. Darkness is following her and she can't shake it. Her heart is good but her choices are poor. Someday she'll listen to me and she will know that I'm not the weakling that she thinks I am. There is so much to say to her if she was open to hearing any of it. I'm waiting in the quietness of the chapel. The vaulted ceiling, the ornate plaster, the patterned tiles, the smell of incense and the sound of the angels coil around me as I dance in the aisle and hold my hands upwards. I do it all the way home and find the doctor coming from number 34.

'What are you doing?' His voice is calm, his walk interested and his head to one side.

'Dancing in the light.'

'I can see that.'

'The angels like it when I dance to their singing.'

He folds his arms across his chest and his eyes sparkle in amusement.

'I need you to keep a secret,' I say.

'Anything for you, Molly.'

'I cannot write and I need to ask you to write to a Dr Brady in Sligo and tell him something for me. Can you do that? Please?'

'Of course. I'd do anything for you, Molly. You know that.'

'Tell him I'll be in the Royal Hospital this coming Friday. I need him to please come to me. I need him to rescue me again.'

'What do you mean?'

'Please write and tell him and mind my money for me too. It's not much but it's all that I have.' I thrust my purse at him. 'Don't tell Peggy. Or anyone, please? I need to trust you.'

'Hospital? Rescue?'

I'm away up and in the door with my sandals making no noise, as he says, 'I'll do all that you ask, Molly. I promise.'

I know that he will, because the shadows have plans. I know he'll not let me down. He'll keep the money no doubt. I can't think about that or about what I have to do next... it must be done. It must be done.

Chapter 43

Peggy has left me be, after hearing from Tess that the sergeant is downstairs. No doubt the sergeant is coming for me, because of Tommy. In the bath, my fingers go wrinkly and I think of when I thought I was melting into the water. Violet and the doctor allowed me to swim on and on and the water was nice on my skin. I still love being clean. The water is clever as it finds all of me. My gramophone plays in the corner, the rose-scented soap is smooth but slips out onto the floor as the words of the song lift me into them.

It won't be as bad as it seems, I tell myself as I slice the skin between my left elbow and wrist. I let the knife run in so that it makes me bleed deep red blood. I dig down on the blade and pull it deeper. It is beyond sore. I bite my lip as the pain becomes unbearable and blood pours into the water. Doing it again is not so easy and the right arm is merely marked. I try it again. The bath's tin clunks when the knife hits off it and the water swirls pink for a while.

I lie back and wait on one life to die and the next to begin. The room goes misty.

The sergeant is here quicker than I thought anyone would be. I'm naked and slippery and he's shouting and heaving me out of the water. Peggy is here now, too, trying to cover me in the towel, worrying about me. Lord love her, the guilt is falling off her with the biggest tears. They think they're stopping the blood from pumping so hard. They're fighting about the time and what to do. The towel is cosy. I'm glad to be covered. I know to stay quieter than I've ever been. The lack of blood makes everything muffled anyhow, the thumping on the stairs, the strange men's fingers digging into my flesh, lifting me, carrying me. I'm bundled, as I always am, into the back seat of a car. It drives quickly, spinning its wheels away from Peggy, from number 34 and all that I know.

I am a fallen woman, and a whore, in the eyes of them all who come to care for me. I'm also a sinner, of an even higher degree. They whisper loudly, 'Tried to do away with herself. She's a whore. Gave her name as Molly McCarthy. She has been in prison as well!'

The gasps off them are loud as they bless themselves and stare at me. It doesn't take long for someone to announce, 'She's that famous healer from Sligo that the priests talked about. Do you remember?'

'She never is?'

'She is! I'm telling ya now that's who she is – "The Red-haired vixen". Remember her?'

'I do! And the papers had her picture. That's her, I'm telling ya.'

Just as I'm starting to panic that the Professor or Vincent will hear of where I am, I see my bearded saviour stride up the corridor towards me. He's pointed in the direction of my bed and he sees me instantly and starts to run.

'Molly darlin',' he breathes into my hair, grabbing me and hurting me in a hug as large as I can take. 'We came as quickly as we could. We're here now.'

It's then I see Violet at his elbow and her mouth is twisted in sadness. There are drops on her cheeks and there are more ready to come. I reach for her hand and she takes mine. She wants forgiveness.

'I am here for you now, Molly. We'll take you home where you belong.'

There's not a need for a word of forgiveness from me. She nods and dabs her nose with a hanky and looks at my bandages.

'I didn't bleed for long,' I tell them. 'Just long enough to get here.'

'Where have you been? The prison didn't know anything, of course, and there was no word. Your father's...'

'Daddy?' I ask them, suddenly fearing he, too, might be behind them. He isn't.

'Michael's fine,' Violet answers. 'He's still drinking, though.'

'Jude?'

'He's grand, but in school. We didn't tell him much... yet.' Violet's words struggle out, 'Jane O'Shea's well. She's back in Violet Cottage, for many months now. She's waiting to see you.'

I catch a good glimpse of the angels' plans for me. My heart soars and I lie back with a sigh. Dr Brady finds a chair and tiny stool. The doctor perches on the stool and looks funny with his knees quite high and his head lower than Violet in her matching tweed jacket and skirt. She's blowing her nose. This wipes away her rouge with each swipe.

'Where have you been? They say you were in a terrible place and there was a mention of trouble with the law again?' Dr Brady leans forward, his beard getting a scratch. 'We tried to find you. Your Aunt Bredagh did too, but then she took off with that Vincent fella.'

Violet pats his arm to silence him. Bredagh gave in to his womanising and wanted his attention. But even she doesn't deserve someone like Vincent.

'Bredagh's in Dublin then?' I squint around them, half-expecting her to march in here with Vincent at her heels. 'I'm better now. I need to get out and away.'

'I'll speak with the doctor and see what's happening.'

Dr Brady's off the stool and it wobbles a little. That leaves Violet and me alone, as the bed's empty beside me.

'I...' she starts. 'I'd no idea what would happen... I'm s–'

'Violet, I have a son in Cavan. I need to get to a ship to take us across an ocean.'

'What?'

'He's called Fionn. He's a healthy boy like Jude.'

'He's...'

'In Cavan. We'll have to go there. I need to get him.'

'But–'

'I know you won't like that I have a child.'

'I–'

'It wasn't a choice of mine. It was forced on me.'

'Oh Molly. That's fierce!'

'There's a woman who is paid to look after him until recently. She knows I'll be back for him.'

Violet is speechless.

'We need to go,' Dr Brady says when he arrives back in a rush. 'The doctor over your care is happy for me to take charge of you. But apparently, the guards will want a word with you. Something about abortions?' He whispers the last word and his eyebrows go very high over his spectacles.

Violet tugs at his sleeve. 'She has a son too, Richard. Our Molly has a son.'

'Peggy,' I mutter. 'It's a woman called Peggy who does the abortions.'

'They think you'd something to do with it.'

'I was in a bad place with bad people. Poor Peggy.'

'Molly wants to get her son, Richard, and to get a ship.' Violet doesn't want me to talk about abortions and definitely doesn't want me to go away again. Her heart is sore at the thought of it. 'Richard?'

Dr Brady is lost in emotion, his lip trembling. His hand searches for mine to hold. He perches on the bed and mumbles, 'Vincent's child?'

'Yes.'

'Sweet Christ, Molly darlin' girl…' He'll rub my skin away with his thumbs if he doesn't stop. 'They never said. Lord love ya, child. We didn't visit as we were told it wouldn't be possible. Did you give birth in prison?'

'No. He was born in number 34 Mountjoy Square. He is a fine boy and is in Cavan.'

'Why must you get a ship? What's all this about?' He looks at the bandages. 'We let this happen to you. We should…'

'Take me away now, please?'

'You're right. Let's get you home.'

Chapter 44

Violet Cottage is just as I remember it. Jude's room has a long train set and many more books in it. They've plumbed an inside bath, sink and toilet, but the house still smells the same. It is musty with a hint of Violet's perfume, smoke and baking. My Jane O'Shea almost squeezes me to death. She sobs and squeezes, then sobs some more.

'Talk is that things were bad for you?' she mumbles. 'We tried to find you. I promise we did.'

'Dr Brady has called a man he trained with in Cavan and we're going there soon,' Violet says over the tea she's pouring. 'He knows of the address you gave us, Molly.'

'It wasn't spelled right.'

'It was good enough.'

'Peggy wrote it for me. I watched it over and over and still it wasn't right, but I know how to get there.'

'This woman, Peggy?' Jane starts.

'Took care of me, as best she could.'

They look at each other. I wonder what they know. How badly will they think of me if they know all that I had to do?

'There's plenty of talk about the place you were in. It's filtered all the way here. Father Sorely knows the priests in Dublin. They're saying that this Peggy Bowden is the one who sold babies to America and…'

'That's her. She's from Sligo, but I don't know from where.'

'I do,' Jane says. 'She's from out near Mayo. Her husband died and she took off to Dublin to be a midwife.'

'That's right.'

I don't like them thinking badly of Peggy. It hasn't been easy to think nice thoughts about her myself but still, I should 'stick up for her' but in doing that I might also make things worse. I'm never good with words.

Violet makes a noise in her throat.

'Was it a whore-house?' Jane asks me outright. She has always loved gossip and wants to know what it was like. She is waiting on me to fill her in.

'It was a whore-house. Yes.'

'That's terrible!' Violet begins and stops herself. 'After all you went through. You didn't have to – please tell me you didn't…'

'I was well-treated… mostly, I was grand.'

Jane cries. Violet starts on about the sins of the flesh and how I'll need to be blessed, churched and confessed to please Father Sorely. 'The things you must have seen, the horrors. I can't imagine the suffering. Oh Molly. I am so sorry.'

'I hurt someone,' I tell them.

Both stop their sobbing and wittering on.

'I cut him like I cut Vincent. I was angry.'

'Oh no!' Jane starts crying again.

'He'll probably tell his mother and she'll make me pay.'

'Prison again? No?' Violet shrieks. 'You can't go back there.'

Jane clutches her hanky to her mouth to stop her making a total fool of herself.

'I was safe in prison.'

Violet paces the floor now and leans with her fingers splayed across Jane's shoulder. They have become closer and rely on one another now. 'There is talk of women going missing from number 34. What else are you running from? The hospital took a lot of convincing to let you out. The worry we have for you is worsening. Lord save us, Molly, what are we to do?'

'I just need to get away from it all. I will to go for the boat as soon as I can.'

'Run away?'

'They won't believe me. No matter what I say.'

Both women know that I'm speaking the truth. Women like me have no power. I've fallen even further in the eyes of everyone. Violet and Jane don't want to think of what I may have had to do to survive in such a place.

'It wasn't that bad in number 34,' I tell their minds. 'The walls looked after me. Peggy did her best with what she was given.'

'You never complain. Never get angry with us.'

'I got angry with Tommy. I was so mad. I needed to get away and have Fionn. I didn't know how I would do it. Poor Tommy.'

'The man you hurt?'

'He made excuses about not helping me.'

'We all did that,' Violet admits.

'I had to help myself.' I lift my bandaged arms. 'I used my gifts to help me.'

'What will this Peggy woman do now?' Jane asks.

'She will probably tell them that I'm to blame and try to run like I did.'

Jane puts down her china cup with a clink into the saucer. 'She wouldn't?'

Violet is back walking the tiled floor.

'Dr Brady will know what to say,' Jane says. 'This Tommy might not do anything.'

'There's a woman missing. Went there to be "seen to" as she was in the family way. What do you know of her, Molly?' Violet asks.

'I know nothing. Peggy came to talk to me in the bath about needing help with something, but I was away with the fairies.'

'Help with what?'

'I don't know. There were bad men starting to come about number 34.'

'I bet there was.' Jane fills up the cups. 'And women, too, no doubt. They can't blame you for anything when you think of the dirty divils that were bound to be there and doing all sorts.'

'Thinking of a dirty divil. Is Bredagh in Sligo?' I ask. 'She's not going to hear that I'm home?'

'She was in Dublin, that's the last we heard about her. Your father's much the same but has lost his job. Bredagh's boys are all doing well for themselves, fair play to them. All got good trades and are hard workers. They don't seem to have much to do with her either. No word at all about what's what with her.'

'When can we go to Cavan?'

'Soon as Richard finishes work and he'll drive.'

'A son?' Jane smiles. 'You brave girl.'

'Fionn. Fionn McCarthy.'

'I don't like that surname now, Jane,' I say. 'I need a new one for my new life.'

'Fionn Brady?' Violet suggests and her eyes brim up. 'You should be a Brady.'

'Molly Brady,' I say it aloud. 'Molly and Fionn Brady.'

It never occurred to me that I should be a Brady – not ever. Now that it's said, it brings a peace with it. Dr Brady bustles in 'What have I missed? I've told them that I'm all finished up for today. Some have only come in for nosiness anyhow. Can Jude stay with you, Jane, while we go to Cavan?'

Violet starts to tell him my long tale of woe. I smile at Jane and sip my tea. Here in Violet Cottage, I finally have a family. I am home. Yet I know in my heart that it will not be my home for long. Life is not good or fair sometimes.

Chapter 45

Once we get to Cavan town, I know how to tell Dr Brady each turn and twist in the road. The laneway to the farm has cattle on it and my patience is thin when we reach the door. A toddler appears with blonde curls and a crust of bread in his fist. He's filthy but smiles at us as we get out of the car. He's all I see but he hides behind the skirt tails talking to Dr Brady and Violet. They're doing the niceties that I should be at. Then the little hand comes out to meet mine and he's back in my arms and has his little nose pushed unto mine.

'Would you look at that?' the big woman says. Her breasts heaving in agony at Fionn coming to me. 'I knew it wouldn't be long until we'd see you.'

'I've to take him now.'

'That was the deal.' Her apron's getting twisted in her hands and Fionn's messy hands are in my hair. 'I'll be fine with it once I know that he's safe.'

She talks at the doctor. 'I'm glad he'll be living with you nice people.' He gives her an envelope of money and shakes her hand over and over. Violet nods and looks around as the woman says, 'He's the best child. Not a bother on him. He gets dirty every day but sure that's what boys should do. I'll miss him.'

'There'll be more people who come. You know nothing of where he is.' My voice is harsh again at her. I do want to hug her tightly and thank her with every ounce of love I have but I have no time for all of that. Instead I go on like Peggy would, 'He's to be safe from bad people now. Please don't say where he is.'

'As long as you let me know in time what's what with him. I've grown so... fond...' Her voice breaks. 'I've toys and clothes you must take…' She goes inside. I can't go with her. I want gone but Violet's nose gets the better of her and she goes in after her to 'help'.

It takes forever for them to come out and I'm in the back seat with Fionn who hasn't taken his eyes off me, or his bread and hands out of my hair. The woman asks for him and I hold him out of the car towards her but pull him back quickly. She might refuse to let me have him. I'm cruel but I can't risk her holding on to him and not letting go. My Fionn doesn't seem to mind when he gets driven away with strangers. He sits on the seat and looks up at me and I promise him, 'You'll have a home now and be safe. I'm your mammy.'

'She was the nicest woman. He's been a lucky boy.' Violet's back is to me. 'She was crying, didn't you notice?'

'I couldn't.'

'We'll have to let her know how he is. She wanted us to wait until her husband was in from the fields. It was harsh of us to leave her like that. It wasn't fair.'

'Life is not fair.' Dr Brady says what I'm thinking. 'Look how Fionn came to Molly and didn't even cry. He's not distressed. He knows his own mother and that woman back there was handsomely paid for looking after him.'

'It's not all about money,' Violet says. 'I'll pray for her and write to her often. Imagine if we lost Jude?'

There's a knot in my stomach. They won't want Jude to leave them. I should have thought of this. I have seen in my dreams that we would all be on the boat together. The Bradys and even Jane are on a large boat, with our hairs blowing in the wind and us standing waving at an empty shore. It's not like me to see things that aren't right. Yes, we are waving goodbye to our old lives and welcoming in the new. Jane has a new hat, Violet has Jude by her side and I've Fionn in my arms.

'I need to get us away. The urges are strong,' I tell them.

'But go where, Molly?' Dr Brady asks. 'Why can't you stay in Violet Cottage? I know the gossip about Fionn will be hard, but we'll manage for a bit.'

'I have to go.'

'Go where?' he asks. 'Where can a lone mother go with a child?'

'I can't heal in Sligo. I can't make life bad for you again. I need to go.'

There is not much talk, as Fionn starts to cry. He nestles into my neck where he used to lie and I hum to him. He sleeps and no-one wants to wake him or talk about us leaving.

Chapter 46

Jude is at a friend's house but will run home soon. Jane is like a cat with kittens. She doesn't know who to get settled in first. Fionn cries when we take him out of the bath and Jane soothes his tears as she dries him. I like to have the past washed off him, and if I'm truthful I'm glad the kisses of another mother are gone too. Violet is all chat about the woman who minded him and how she must be heart-sore. I can't answer her, as I can't let that guilt in. I simply can't take on more sorrow.

Jane says, 'I'm away home,' and she waves back to us, all the way to the gate. Dinner is a lovely roast, usually served on Sundays at midday but we're all hungry. Fionn lies across my lap and plays with a toy wooden tractor.

'The child is nothing like his father. He's so like Jude,' Violet mutters. My fork cracks off my plate as I flap it down with annoyance.

Dr Brady grits his teeth at me and smiles. He would never give out to her.

'Do you ever cry, Molly?' Violet asks me. 'You only cried the night you came here and the time... Vincent...'

'DON'T!'

I shock Fionn. He holds his hands over his ears like I do.

'Don't mention that beast again.'

Violet continues eating. My shout didn't bother her much. 'I just want to know what goes on in your head?'

'I'm not a halfwit.'

Dr Brady's mouth is full and he tries to come between us with some words.

'I know that!' Violet says quickly. 'I just mean your son is home and you are safe and you barely flinch.'

163

'What can I do other than say thank you? I said it twice.'

Violet doesn't look like she remembers it.

'I'm grateful to you both,' I say.

'I don't want you to feel obliged in any way,' Violet says amid mouthfuls and slurps at her milk. 'Richard and I have talked about this. We want to keep Fionn here, even if you cannot stay. We are getting on in years, but with Jane we'll manage. Jude will love him and be a great help.'

Dr Brady's eyes won't meet mine. His air is on fire with worry. I can tell that Violet does mean well. She's trying to find a way of me bettering my reputation if that's at all possible.

'Wherever you go, you won't need to be known as a… well, you don't want Fionn to be a…'

'Bastard?' I ask her.

'Molly, don't use those words.'

'That's what you mean?'

'Yes. But not in front of the child.'

'He's almost sleeping now.' Fionn is like a rag doll across my lap, breathing peacefully, his tractor in his fist resting on the dining chair next to us.

'No matter where you go there will be questions, about you being alone, with a child.'

'I'll say that his father was an animal and forced me—'

'Dear God, I hope that child is asleep.'

'Fionn will never leave me again. Ever.' I start to eat and the conversation stops until the clock in the hall starts to chime that it's seven.

'Eating at this hour of the night will give us heartburn,' Dr Brady says. 'It was worth all those miles to see your son.'

'Thank you for Dublin and for today.'

He nods at me as Violet starts to stack the plates and take her temper out on them. When she's out of the room and on the way to the kitchen I go to move.

'Don't disturb his sleep.'

'I must help her. She'll get crosser.'

'Violet is only thinking of a solution. But, if the guards were to call and ask questions, we might have some bother explaining where he came from. I'll say to her that all that will take too much time to sort things. That you need to go soon and will have to take him with you.'

'I do need to take him with me.'

'Were things that bad in Dublin?'

'I don't need people to find me. I need to go somewhere where I can figure this out.'

'Scotland or England?' Dr Brady suggests. 'It's across the sea, but not too far? The men go over and back to the potato picking and the building work. There's many a hard worker around here who could help us find you a place.'

There is a light in my soul at that suggestion.

'We'll get you a worn wedding ring that fits and with a new name, Molly Brady, a good few pounds in your purse, and a place to live, you'll be fine. I've contacts over there and there'll be no need to work for a while at least. We could visit?'

He's making my head sore with the plans. I rub my temple and a tear drops when I lean forward. Another comes and another as I see a feather at my feet. 'Thank you. The angels are happy too.'

Chapter 47

'No church or law-man needs to know anything at all.' Jane is lecturing Violet in the kitchen. 'No-one needs to tell them a thing.'

Jude never left my side all night and even when I had to put Fionn to bed in the little bed set up in his room, he came, too, and insisted I sleep in his bed and he'd sleep on the floor. He is tall now as I look at him in the long breeches he wears. He's complaining about having to go to school, which I'm told is unusual but he wants to be with us. I wonder, has anyone told him we won't be here long.

'Don't be gossiping about me being here when you're at school.' I fix his collar and pull his jacket on him. 'I don't want people knowing that I'm here.'

'Why? Is it cause you have a baby?'

'Yes.' I can't lie to him like everyone else does. 'I don't want my father to know anything.'

'Right. But you'll be here when I get back?'

'But we go tomorrow. I'm getting a lift in a truck taking men back to London.'

'You gonna build the roads too?' He shows me his teeth with the laughing he's doing. 'Why can't you stay?'

'I can do my healing over there. You'll come visit.'

His arms circle my waist and he hugs me tight into my cheek and then is gone like lightning out the door and down the lane. 'He's a great runner.'

'He's the best son a woman could ask for,' Violet says. 'We're blessed.'

'He has always been blessed.'

Fionn is hungry and Jane spoon-feeds him. Although both Fionn and I want to do it, I know she's enjoying it.

'We wanted to have you here full-time as a child too, Molly. We did,' Violet says.

'It's fine now.'

'What's past is done,' Jane says, trying to ease the tension. 'Dr Brady's writing that letter of introduction to someone he knows in Cricklewood. I know a lady who runs a shop over there. She used to anyhow. Half of Ireland lives in London.'

'Bredagh and Vincent are in Dublin, aren't they?' I ask.

'There's been changes in the "Big Smoke" with the newspapers talking about the shooting of some bad boyos. Vincent is up to no good in the capital: he'd need to watch himself.'

'I've prayed that he'll die.'

Violet doesn't give out, even she can see why I would wish such things. 'One bad man I know has died in Dublin recently. But the beast is still alive.'

'Are you sure?' Jane asks.

I touch my heart and my head. She understands me.

'It might not be long, though, if things are bad in Dublin?' Jane says.

'There has been mention of that American criminal Larry Sheeran in the papers. He's found a long-lost daughter. They mentioned it's a Peggy Bowden and that she's helping to nurse him now,' Violet says, shuffling out a paper that she gets sent with the postman. There's not too many papers sent to the local post office and sometimes she gets them many days late and goes off her head about it. 'There's no photograph, which is a pity. I do remember the last time she was all over the papers. She was so pretty! And her a Sligo woman?'

I don't remind her that Peggy's also a criminal.

Jane leans in over the rustling sheets, too, and is squinting. 'Imagine? Is she your Peggy, do you think, Molly? If she is, then she's the daughter to that Larry Sheeran who was run out of Dublin. Years ago. They were only letting him back to die on

Irish soil. Your Peggy's probably out of the frying pan into the fire, getting caught up in all of this.' She taps her finger on the paper on the table. 'Your angels got you out of Dublin just at the right time. I'd want nothing to do with the likes of that fellow Larry Sheeran. Family means nothing to the likes of him. I'd say he's behind those shootings in Glasnevin. He's looking to get his Dublin back.'

'Peggy can take care of herself,' I say. 'It hasn't taken her long to get in the papers and escape number 34. She's living with him now, isn't that what the papers said?'

'Nursing him.'

'She was looking to get away for a while too.'

'But you had to cut yourself to escape her,' Jane says. I pull the sleeves on my blouse down. 'She must be some hard dolly bird! But even she doesn't need to be involved with the likes of that Larry. They say he eats children.'

Violet laughs and I do giggle. It is Jane's fanciful way of putting things that lifts the mood in the kitchen.

'They do.' She laughs a little at it herself. 'He's a bad apple or egg or something rotten.'

'At least Peggy won't be looking for me. She'll be busy.'

'We'll keep an eye and ear out as to where Bredagh is too.' Jane squeezes my shoulder when passing. 'But word is that she has fallen a long way from where she was when she had you working all the hours God sent. She's whoring somewhere–' Violet silences her with a glare. 'She's not doing so well. She's busy too.'

'You could try to stay here…' Violet starts just as there's a knock on the front door. We can hear the rapping all the way to the back of the house.

'That is the guards looking to question me. I don't like anyone to lie… but I think you should say that I'm not here.'

'I'll go,' Jane says, wiping her hands in her apron. 'Lock that back door and keep that child quiet. I'll lie to these boys and be back in a minute.'

Chapter 48

'You were right, Molly. It was the law-men!' Jane's been given a whiskey by Violet to calm her nerves. It is in the good crystal and Violet never pours a whiskey so it is a big one. 'They wanted to speak to you or know where you were and Dr Brady too. I said that the doctor's up at the big house but they were looking about knowing what happened to that fellow Tommy and some woman called Dot McKenzie.'

'The missing woman?' Violet whispers.

'The poor woman's definitely been seen at number 34 Mountjoy Square and since she's gone missing and you've gone missing as well, they're asking questions. They said they'd come back to ask the doctor as he's in charge of ya.'

'Oh my,' Violet gasps.

'I said that you were here for a night, but that you ran away and we've no idea where you are. I said Mrs Brady was in bed since with the worry.' Jane winks and cackles. 'I should be on the stage.' She cackles again. 'The doctor won't be worried about it. Sure, what can he do if you ran off? Like our Jude, you're some runner.' The giggles out of her are funny. I laugh too. 'It's the whiskey,' she tells Violet. 'Why am I talking to you? Sure, you're in your bed with the worry. There's no point in talking to you.'

'You're an awful woman. They'll think I have a nervous condition now.'

This makes Jane chuckle again and then start to choke on a mouthful. It sprays into the air and Fionn gurgles.

Even Violet laughs as Jane slaps her knee in glee. Wiping her eyes she says, 'It is good to laugh. But do you know anything about that McKenzie woman?'

'Not a thing.'

'There's nothing to fear then, the truth will out,' Jane says and slurps more big mouthfuls into her.

'We'll be gone early. They have done their duty now but they'll be back. I hope the doctor will be all right? I don't want to cause him any trouble after all he's done for us.'

'No-one turns the word in a doctor's mouth,' Jane says. 'Sure, he's a god about here. If he says something then, we all think that it's truer than the Bible. Especially since you've been away. Dr Brady's a fine doctor and he's been building up a nice business. Everyone loves our Dr Brady.'

She starts on the hiccups then and our sides are sore laughing at her.

***

Jane's wedding ring fits my finger. I refuse to take it at first, but she insists. 'A band to protect your honour until we meet again. I'd be proud to let you wear it.'

Dr Brady fills my purse with notes and many of his letters of recommendation and explanation line my handbag. I practice saying and looking at the address in Cricklewood. Oddly it's number 340 Cricklewood Broadway, London. 'Not far from The Crown pub, apparently,' Dr Brady says pushing his glasses up onto his lovely nose. 'Near Gladstone Park. Short walk for you Molly to take Fionn to green spaces. There's many Irish there and a big dance hall. You must to go to it as well – dance and have fun. Meet people.'

Violet is standing back to let me out the front door. She has already hugged me and Fionn and nudged Jude to stop crying. He wipes his nose with his sleeve and she doesn't give out to him and takes his arm instead and both smile as I wave back with Fionn's little hand. Dr Brady holds the truck door open and helps me up into the dark space between two burly men and hands me in Fionn. They 'hullo' and shift in their seats and one takes Fionn for me. I get comfortable and ask the angels to not let me cry. Our suitcase is tucked in somewhere and the door gets a bang. The engine revs off and we are again leaving.

The men are full of chat after telling me their names. They talk about the fine son I have and the great 'head of hair and fine teeth' we both have. There's a lovely atmosphere in the small space. They're not sad to be finding work, only lonesome to be leaving home. They go for months, sometimes years at a time, but they are sure that they will be back. One of their first questions is if we will need a lift back and I truly don't know.

I sleep much of the way to the boat and so does Fionn. We board with a line of people and walk about and stretch the legs as the boat surges up and down. The wind whistles my hair around me and I don't go near the railings in case Fionn would fall in. My stomach lurches, too, and I'm tired. It doesn't take long for us to be back into another truck for a big drive. The darkness hides the world we're in now, but there's a busyness even in the night and it makes me happy for once to be surrounded in people. Fionn is not as settled as he usually is and each man takes it in turns to amuse him and I snooze a bit until I wake myself up from snoring. All the men are married and I am not worried about them being so close. There's a sing-a-long for a time and I join in, 'When Irish eyes are smiling…'

'You can sing, my girl,' the man driving says.

'Thanks.'

The talk comes around to Dublin and the goings-on with men killing each other. 'The world has gone mad. They say that Larry Sheeran's not as sick as he made out. He got to come back to Dublin because he wanted to die on Irish soil and now they say that he's not dying at all. He has already taken over the whole of his side of the Liffey River. Has some family back now with him and all the rest of the city is running scared.'

Peggy is making a name for herself already, I can feel it.

No-one asks me about Fionn's father but I've seen some of them look at Jane's ring. They're local men who I've no doubt met over the years at the healing, but none pretend to know me or my situation. They don't seem to be judging me either. Irish men ask questions and I know that they will before long. Sure enough, one does mention my own father. 'Michael's not a bad fellow you know, Molly. Your father I mean. The drink is a curse and with your mother dying so young and the doctor taking in your brother… He'd little to live for after that brother of his was bad to you. We all know he was bad to you.'

'Yes,' I tell him and wave to Fionn who's now with the man who's driving and looking over at me. I'm glad they know the truth of things.

'They say you don't talk much.'

'I don't.'

'Me mother always said if you've nothing good to say, then say nothing.' His teeth are bad but he laughs all the same. 'They'll be no-one thinking badly of you in Cricklewood, if we've anything to do about it anyhow. You're a fine lassie. We'll tell the priest that we knew your husband.'

'Thank you.'

Everyone in the truck knows I've never had a husband and probably never will.

'We'll send people to you for the healing too,' one fellow says. 'Pay no heed to anyone who tells you not to be doing it. You must. There'll be lots of people looking to have the old ways around them and to be cured rather than going to the English doctors. Some of them won't look at us anyhow. You'll be rolling in money!'

'I know.'

They all laugh at my confidence.

'It's not about the money. I'm going to be a great woman,' I tell them when they stop laughing. 'Thank you for being good to us. I'll not forget it.'

Chapter 49

Cricklewood is a fine place. The rooms I've taken are above a grocer's and he is a fine widowed man who says that his shop is open all hours of the day and well into the night. He offers me a job, too, if I need it. Considering the signs in other windows, 'No blacks, no dogs and no Irish,' he is generous.

But the first morning, when I waken after only a few hours' sleep, there are a few people standing under the small window in the busy street. I pull up the sash to hear, 'You that Molly Brady? The healer? We're all waiting to see ya.'

The door out onto the street is separate from the shop and the stairs go straight into my little kitchen. There is a bedroom directly off it into the back of the building with no outside space for us, but Fionn toddles from the kitchen to the bedroom and around the few pieces of simple furniture. A tiny privy is tucked in under the stairs with a tiny door in the bottom hallway. Racing out the bedroom door, I fall over one man sitting waiting in the stairway. In my nightdress, I'm scarlet red when he lifts me. There are three more behind him and all are waiting on me. My life in Cricklewood is starting before I can even take a piss.

With my overcoat on I wash in the bucket in the privy and pull on my best dress and buff my shoes with newspaper on the peg. Slipping back up past all the people waiting, I put on the kettle on the little stove and usher in the first person. He is a tall, broad man who has headaches. My hands go into his hair and it doesn't take long for him to sigh into my hands. Fionn plays all the while, sucking and gnawing on a crust of bread the grocer left up to us. The milky tea spills from the mug I gave him as he walks around the floor but on and on I go, healing each person as best

I can. It's only eleven and I'm done with the queue at the door and have a tin full of donations that the people give to Fionn. He doesn't mind that I take the money from his little grubby grip.

'Blessings to the child. What a good child he is.'

My heart is at peace in Cricklewood. The walls of the two-storey building are firm and will protect us. The streets are full of Irish people. I can 'spot them a mile away'. The cut of their dress or the caps on the men, the walk or the accent, the nods and the hullos. Here, though, I hold my head high and fear no-one. The park is green as far as the eye can see and there are trees as tall as houses and as broad as roads. The traffic doesn't bother me like it bothered me in the early days in Dublin and the weather is pleasant with a breeze that blows with a welcome in its tail. Fionn's feet drag under his little tired legs, so I carry him nestled into my neck all the way home. I'm about ready to cry with tired joy at our new life when I see the man I fell over on the stairs earlier sitting on a bench not far from our door. He's not Irish and is waiting on me.

'Can I help?' he asks me. His face is covered in stubble, dark like his hair and his brown eyes shine from under his soft cap. He thrusts it back on his head with calloused hands and then stands with it on his hip, smiling at us both. I like the heavy weight of Fionn in my arms and never want to let him go again.

'No thank you. Your headache is better?'

'It went like "puff",' his accent sings to me. He is not an Englishman. 'The whole place says how good you are. I'll take boy, he how you say? … Big for small boy and small arms.'

'Could you open the door? There's a key on a string inside the letter box.'

'I know.' He pulls the string and unlocks the door following me up the stairs and into our new home, taking the string and key with him. When he was here earlier I'd been distracted and hadn't noticed how tall and handsome he is. He likes the look of me too. He's uncomfortable and shuffles his hands into his pockets, he's not sure he should be near my bed. Fionn gets tucked in and I kiss his little nose.

'You're alone?' he says, looking around.

'Yes.'

'I might ask you… I might take you,' his accent sings almost. 'I take you to… Meet people? You dance? Yes?'

'I don't know.'

'You must dance? Sing?'

'I'm only here since late last night.'

'I don't want other man to ask you.' His teeth are in a perfect row of white squares and his lips are full and grinning. 'I heard you were in Cricklewood. I had to come see. Something in here,' he points to his stomach, 'told me to come.'

'You work fast.'

He misunderstands me, as he starts, 'I work hard. Build for the film sets. You come see? Say yes?' I point at Fionn and before I can say anything, 'Bring the bambino.'

'I might.'

'The men they say you sing. I love to sing,' and he starts a song and stumbles over the English words. '*Rain, rain, don't go away, it's so posie in the rain…*'

'*Cosy in the rain, pitter patter on the pane…*' I know the song and sing with him for a few lines. Our voices are nice together.

'Bella. You beautiful. The talk, it is right.'

'There's been plenty of gossip about me?' I laugh and point to the one hard chair by the small kitchen table and make us a pot of tea as he mentions my dead husband. I can't tell him it is a lie as he goes on that I'm a healer from Sligo, Ireland, by the name of Brady.

'You know plenty.'

'All the people they say you special? That you see… angels? My Nonna she die and on her dying she said she'd send me, how you say… a girl with fire hair. A hair, red girl.'

The shadows are dancing, distracting me and making my eyes flit about.

'Did she say about my son?'

'No.' He's not bothered by Fionn and smiles on at me.

'I don't have a husband. I never married.'

'Oh.' He smiles and then gulps at the mug.

'I'm hoping Fionn's father never finds me.'

'Sì.'

'I'm good in my heart. A good woman.'

'Sì.'

'I don't like to talk much.'

'I talk all time.'

'I've been in prison.'

This stops him slurping at the tea. He leaves the mug down. The shadows are hoping that I shut up.

'I'm hiding in Cricklewood.'

'From police?'

'Maybe.'

He doesn't look worried or like he may run away. 'But all people know you are here.'

I shrug. 'Sure, what can I do?'

'I'm Italian. I not like police.'

I lean against the table and look down at him. From the top of his thick dark hair to the bottom of his working boots, he is a fine man. There's no question that he's a good, strong, hard-working man.

'I make a beard,' he says. 'It nice, yes?' His fingers rasp across his square jaw and his perfect teeth appear again in his sallow skin.

'The angels told me to look out for a man with a beard. They said that he'd rescue me. That he'd fill my soul.'

'Soul?'

How do I explain it? I touch my heart, my head and then my lips.

He thrusts out his hand with the dirty nails and says, 'Molly Brady, Luca Giovanni Romano. My soul, it need you.'

My hand is in his and when he leaves I find a tiny white feather on his seat.

Chapter 50

The better days start. Letters come from Jane, Violet and Dr Brady. Jude sends an odd one when he is made to write. I can tell he is forcing the news out onto the paper. Growing up, he has no time with all his own school work and God knows what. I can't read and neither can Luca but I smell the paper and wait until someone who can read comes for the healing. I ask them to read them to me, as payment. I can hear all the Brady's and Jane O'Shea talk through the words. For the first time, I understand why people read and write.

I'm always laying my hands on people. On and on they come. The more I do it, the stronger I get. My wounds have healed quickly and I can roll up my sleeves to care for Fionn and the callers to 340 Cricklewood Broadway. It is like the whole of the past is fading like my scars.

There are no thoughts of Vincent or Bredagh.

Peggy and Daddy enter my thoughts sometimes and I pray for them. My mornings can be full of people coming and Fionn plays happily or naps. I can't help watching him breathe when I'm alone with him. Sometimes long into the night, I watch his little chest move up and down and see his eyelids flutter. My hands slip over him taking the temper tantrums away. They come sometimes when he needs me and I'm busy. There is nothing of his father in him. Nothing at all, and he hums along when I sing now. We have fresh food a few steps from the door and I barely pay for a thing as the grocer loves Fionn. He has no children and chucks at Fionn's chin.

Sometimes the fellows from the truck call in to talk of home and to bring injured men to see me. Scaffolders fallen from great heights are beyond my healing powers and I go to them sometimes and shake my head. Many others have battered skulls, busted fingers, bruising or aching joints and call to me. The battered Irishmen queue outside The Crown, not far away, and wait on the ganger. These souls wait on him to nod or pick them 'for the start', to pick and shovel all day.

A foreman needed me when he fell into the ditch six-foot deep and someone didn't throw the rubble back but forward on top of him. It was me, rather than a doctor that the other foremen asked to look at him. He survived and I told him that he 'just needed his tongue tied for a while'. He listened, as he was never unfortunate enough to fall again. Ever since I healed him, I have had a stream of men coming from all over London, with notes from gangers and foremen asking me to heal this and that, to get them back to work. I give the notes to the grocer and he collects the pay.

'Paddys with shovels are better than the Germans!' I've heard it said and although some are ashamed by their dirty hands and boots, there is a pride in most of them about the building up of a destroyed city. They are my best source of income.

Since I've come here, Fionn never leaves my sight. A happiness has blossomed in me that I can't explain. I fill my lungs with it. Every morning I waken and lean into Fionn to waken him and he smiles at me. There's nothing better in this world than his smile, nothing better until he laughs or hums along with me.

One woman who comes for the healing always has a toothache. I explain that I can't pull out teeth. 'Take the pain away until it falls out,' she states as if it is so easy. I take the pain away and she comes back offering to look after Fionn for me. Her hair is thinning and her mouth is laden with rotten teeth. 'We all know that lovely Italian calls to take you dancing. You must go. Live while you are pretty and young.'

She is a good woman, called Mary and she has twelve grown-up children, who she tells me all about. I sense she also knows the Bradys and she is like an earthly guardian angel they've sent to watch over us.

'I'll stay here where Fionn knows, until you come home. Go now, get ready. I read books and can be content until you come home.'

I watch her take a book from her bag.

'Go get ready. He'll take you out if he sees you dressed for dancing.'

Something in me wants to go. I long to dance with Luca.

'Mary say we go dancing?' Luca swings me with him when I appear into the kitchen. Booky Mary is delighted with herself and so am I.

Luca skips down the stairs and runs around me like a puppy. Many people know us well and men bob their caps and the women smile. He swings his hand into mine and he tells anyone on the way to the dance hall that is where we are going.

'I'm happy,' I tell him. His lips hit mine with a smack. Right there in the street he folds his arms around me and smacks his lips against mine again. His stubble is hair now and it scratches me. I like it against my cheek as he nuzzles into my neck and I wriggle free. 'Don't. Not here.'

He always listens to me and wants to please me. Without a complaint, he holds my hand all the way to the Galtymore Dance Hall.

The music is loud but lively. Choking smoke stings my eyes while I sip on the lemonade Luca buys for me. The round tables rock a bit if you lean on them and there is a stickiness to the floor. A few familiar faces, red with the heat, nod their welcome. There is a band on a raised stage with lights on it. They are battering out *The Walls of Limerick* and the floor pounds with the people all following a routine they know without thinking. I've never seen the likes of it. An odd time as a little girl, I watched a small group take to the floor in McLaughlin's in Collooney but this makes me excited to just watch. The whole place moves to the music and everyone is enjoying themselves. Laughing, the women leap and cross over and through arms of the men, and they all look happy. It is good to be in such air.

'We'll calm things down now,' the man on the stage says standing forward. 'When Irish eyes are smiling...'

'It's Dr Brady's song,' I tell Luca.

He's been sitting staring at me. 'I look at you all night. Forever, I look at you.'

I know what he means. That is what I do to Fionn. I love to watch him be happy.

When the band play a waltz, Luca holds me in his strong arms and steps with me showing me what we should do. I've never done it before but by the third song in the same rhythm I'm not looking at my feet. He whispers, 'One, two, three,' into my ear. His breath tickles me and puts my feet in the wrong direction. He loves to hold me tighter then. Luca makes me tingle like Tommy did. More than Tommy did. It's been a long time since I thought of Tommy.

'I sing,' Luca says and stops my memories. 'They ask me. This song I sing for you.'

He is on the stage in a flash and I'm on the floor with people standing cheering, clapping and stomping, delighted to see my Luca is about to sing.

The world stops.

He is up there away from me, but he keeps sticking his arm out towards me. 'Which way did my heart go, from me straight to you. Which way did my heart go? One look and I knew, that I was yours forever, my search for love was over...'

I am mortified! Struck to the spot on the dance floor. I've never heard a voice like it. Deep and smooth, his Italian accent sings loud and clear. The words are sometimes slurred as he is not sure if they are the right English ones. But, those words are all for me. My face is like a beetroot, I know it must be. I hold my ears, I know people are looking. Are they laughing? No. They love his singing. On he goes. He likes being in everyone's ears. On his voice goes, telling me and everyone else of his love for me. It is beautiful but through my fingers I listen and stare at the wooden floor hoping he'll stop soon. I want to sit down and be alone with him.

The whole place claps and roars at him to sing more and someone nudges me. Luca is calling me towards him with his hands. I get shoved towards the stage and I'm lifted up the steps along the side and whooshed across the stage. 'When Irish eyes are smiling…'

Nobody minds that we start singing that song again. The full room roars along and I think the roof might come off. Luca's heart yearns to make me happier. I'm not sure I could feel more alive, more content.

I close my eyes, hold my head back and sing loud and long. Suddenly, I notice there is no-one else singing. Luca has silenced them all, and they and he urge me to sing on. I can't. My words stop. He sings the next words with me and then gets more silent waiting for me to go on. I try to please him and sing to the end of the verse. The people shout, whistle and clap and I hold my ears again. Luca's arms lift me up and into them and he swirls me around to more clapping. I think I'll die from blushing.

'Italians have no shame,' he tells me on the way home when I've slapped him and told him off. 'You need to be heard and seen. Beautiful Molly Brady cannot be hidden away in rooms in the dark. You need to be… in the light. Like a flower…' he starts all this fancy talk in his 'broken English' as the grocer calls it and I love him for loving me.

'Next Saturday, we go again? Yes?'

I find myself agreeing without thinking if the Booky Mary lady will mind Fionn again.

'Course I will. You are in love. You need this happiness,' she tells me as she puts her book into her bag and is away with a kiss to Fionn's sleeping head. 'We all deserve to be happy. Let it in, my dear. Let it in.'

Chapter 51

The letters from home come now with slips of the newspaper in them. I ask Booky Mary to read them for me. 'I could teach you to read,' she says. I hand her a slip of note paper from Jane, fancy paper from Violet and a scribble from Dr Brady, which she usually can't make out for ages.

The newspaper clippings tell us about the rise of badness in the capital. There are not too many names mentioned, but Sheeran stands out. Sergeant Bushell who used to call to number 34 is dead after a bad beating. Peggy's photo comes with one letter. She is standing in a fancy gown, with a glass in her hand in the ambassador's residence in the Phoenix Park. Times sure have changed for the bold Peggy. Am I glad? I don't know how I am about it.

Then one day, there is only a thin bit of the newspaper in an envelope with a short note in Jane's handwriting.

'Vincent McCarthy has died,' Booky Mary tells me. 'This is his death notice.'

There are no clues given in the paper but Jane's note tells me that he was killed for being a criminal boyo in Dublin. There is no word of Bredagh but she's been missing for a long while and a woman's corpse was found in the canal. Jane thinks what I think, that Bredagh is gone too. Mary sympathises with me, 'I'm sorry for your trouble. But it sounds like he was not the best egg in the basket. And I know Bredagh's disappearance will hit you hard, too, my love. Stay strong, though, the world is changing and you need to shine. Be careful but enjoy your new life.'

'He was my uncle on one side of the family and she was my aunt on the other,' I tell Booky Mary when she stops reading Jane's words and wipes her nose.

'Is this Vincent the one they say you went to prison over?' There is no disgust in her voice. 'A woman needs to protect herself. I had a man once who needed a knife stuck in him, only I hadn't the gumption.' Mary gets to her feet to put Fionn into our bed for me.

'Thank you, Mary.'

'It's not right that I have to read your private letters.'

'I'll never read nor write. I've other gifts.'

'You are a wonderful mother and that is one of the best gifts you can give.'

Vincent is not in the light. Of that I am certain. As hard as it is to understand where souls go, his is wiped out. He might be burning. He will never be at peace. It is clear to me that I am free now.

'My Fionn must never know or be like his father,' I pray. Yet, it is an empty wish. It will be hard to keep Fionn from his nature and I can't change his blood. I cry a little with a mother's worry.

Luca is always mad for dancing. He jigs out on the street, before we get to the Galtymore Dance Hall. He's full of life and good humour. I love being near him, can't wait to see him and long for him to look at me the way he does. He never promises me anything or gets angry with me. I've no need to give him a part of me, although I do want to.

'We must be married,' he says when I tease him. 'Take off that ring,' he says as we dance a slow waltz together. 'It is not a right ring.'

The teasing from folks is fierce, I know others mock about making an honest woman of me.

'My family – I get Booky Mary to write and tell them about you,' he says. 'I say, Irish girl, red hair, I love her. Do you love me?' When he is tickling my neck and whispering in my ear, I almost burst with the love in me for him. 'Tell me you feel it? You do?' His hand puts mine on his heart and there it beats over and over. I seep all the love I have in me into his chest. His nose touches mine. The whiskey on his lips meet mine and neither of us care if anyone sees.

We sing most nights together. Sometimes a country song, other times an Irish or a simple Italian folk song and an odd time, I'll sing alone.

'No-one speaks when you sing,' Luca says. 'You were born to do it.'

I think of how I've always been singing but didn't know that I was. For me, it was to heal myself, sort out the badness around me, to melt me away from the world. I'd never heard much music until I came to London. Yes, the Professor bought me a gramophone and somehow he knew that I'd love it, but it only had two records. Dr Brady sang and I heard the wireless sometimes but he'd turn it off to talk to me. I was only wanting to listen to it and go over the waves it made in my mind.

'I've been on the sea, but I couldn't look at it,' I say to Luca on the way home. 'Fionn was in my arms and I didn't want the deep water to take him.'

'We'll go to the ocean soon,' he says. 'Yes?'

'Please. I want to take Fionn to the seaside. I dream of it.'

'In Italy the sun, the sand it all is beautiful. Someday, I take you there.'

My healing is going well and yet it is making me very tired. I only go out now to be alone with Luca, but I would far rather sleep. My stash of cash is big. That is all that I know. I have no wants for anything. The grocer is suggesting I place my money in a bank. I am not keen on that and as he keeps it for me, I don't think I need to worry. I can't count it well and need him and Luca to keep me right. If Peggy was here she'd tell me I was mad to trust men, and she may be right, but I have little choice. I must believe that the better times are here for me now. Like always, though, I worry about when and how the better times will end.

'All good things come to an end,' I tell Booky Mary when she asks me why I'm so glum.

'Luca loves you. He will ask you to marry him any day now. He's saving up because he knows how much you earn. He needs to provide for you when you stop working.'

'I'll never stop the healing,' I tell Mary as she tidies Fionn's toys into the old orange crate and her books into her shopping net. 'I need to do my healing.'

'A man like Luca might not let you,' she says and lets herself out the door with a 'Good-night now.'

I don't sleep well, tossing and turning, thinking and worrying. It isn't like me to fret about the future. I live like a dog does, wandering from one feed and moment to the next. Loving loyally as best I can no matter what the kicking I get is like. The shadows, of course, are in my hair with their long fingers, telling me all will be well and that there is a plan.

I try to believe them. Fionn snores and cuddles in his new soft bear. I thank the stars that he has none of the worries I had as a child. I talk to myself and watch him sleep and offer all my worries up and away from me.

'What will be will be,' I tell the night. 'There is no point in going up to meet the rain.'

I see myself with Luca and feel the sand in my toes and the water racing in to meet me. All will be grand if I just let in the love. All will be fine if I believe I deserve the best.

Chapter 52

It is Jude's handwriting on the envelope. I race all the way to where Booky Mary lives and thump on her door.

'It's the doctor,' she tells me. 'I can read it word for word to you. But it is your doctor friend. He's very sick and Jude wants you to come home and heal him. He says the others didn't want to tell you, but he wants you to come home. The doctor does too.'

'I just knew something was brewing. I felt something coming, Mary, but I didn't want to think about it.'

Mary shudders.

'I must go home to him.'

'But if he's going to die, is there any point? It's not all that easy to get across that short stretch of ocean. Should you go back if you are avoiding trouble?'

'I need to give him a safe death. I need to be with him as he goes into the light.'

Mary holds on to my hand and squeezes. 'Will you do that for me when it's my time?' she asks, showing me her rotten teeth.

'I may die before you, Mary,' I say, and am not sure why I do.

Her tut-tuts could be heard in Cork.

The Irish lads in the truck will be different men than the ones I travelled with before, but I don't care. Booky Mary offers to keep Fionn but I know that Jane and Violet will want to see him, and I can't leave him behind me ever again.

'Isn't it bad to go?' Luca begs. 'The police?'

'By the sound of the slips of newspaper coming from Ireland, they've more to bother them these days.'

'But this Peggy?'

'She needs me too. I can tell.'

He sighs a big sigh. 'I don't like you going.'

'I'll be back.'

'Marry me?'

'No.'

'Marry me?' His handsome brow is all furrowed. 'I need to know you'll come back. I know you find it hard to say you love me, but in time you will. Marry me?'

'No.'

'Come...'

'I'll come back.'

He lifts me into the truck, warning the men, 'She's my woman. Leave her be.' He leans up and in and kisses me square on the mouth, then both cheeks. He holds my face in his palm and slips his tongue in making a spectacle of us and stirring the place between my legs something shocking.

The men whistle and mock as he slams the door and thumps the truck, for it to go, before he changes his mind.

'He's not happy at you leavin',' one of them says and Fionn waves at the busy London street. 'Aren't you the healer woman?'

'I am.'

It's then they all start with every ailment they've ever had and it is no time until we're on the ocean. The waves lash the boat and the storm makes me sick. Vomiting, I try not to frighten Fionn. He seems to love the sea and wanders out onto the deck, hand in hand with some of the younger men who aren't tired of children. The drive to Sligo is a miserable one with me dry heaving into a bucket. The men tease me that I can't heal myself of what's wrong with me. They suspect I'm pregnant, but I'm not. There has been no man since Dublin. I try to sleep when Fionn does and I don't know it until we are pulling into Ballisodare village and up the lane to Violet Cottage.

Jane is out and has us both inside by the range with sugary, milky tea in us, before I can blink. She is all chat about the doctor's sickness coming on for a long time.

'Violet ignored all the signs and is off at some church gathering, about f-ing flowers.' Jane says and then whispers ever so softly,

'I think it's the consumption or something worse that we can't mention. He caught it from his patients. But don't say I said that now.'

'I see.'

'He's wasted away and is in a pile of pain. The poor divil. No matter what he takes. Not even the poteen helps. 'Tis bad.'

'Violet's at the church every hour that God sends. Sure, what use is that?' Jane smiles at Fionn picking his nose. 'What a fine boy. You look wrecked, Molly.'

'I've been working.'

'Healing?'

'Aye.'

'Word has been getting back here that you are one famous woman in London. And that you're singing now on a stage, no less?'

I hadn't mentioned that to anyone in my letters. Would Mary have written it without me knowing? It is a shameful secret, one that I enjoy, but one that I'm embarrassed about liking all the same.

'Tell me now about this Italian, before you up to see the doctor?'

'There's nothing to tell.'

'Is he handsome?'

I think of my fine Luca.

'Is he good to you?'

'The best. And to Fionn too.'

'What's up with him then? You aren't hitched?'

'Nothing.'

'Does he smell of that garlic? That stinks. They say them foreigners smell of it.'

'He smells nice.'

'Is he dark-skinned?'

'Yes.'

'Everywhere?' she asks me with a chuckle.

'I don't know.'

'Arah now girl, it's been months since you mentioned him first. There's no Violet here now to be tutting her disapproval. We all know Italians are like stallions.'

She always makes me laugh. 'I missed you, Jane. He wants to wait until we're married. Do things right.'

'Of course! And he'll be lucky to have you.'

'I've a bad temper and he is a good man.'

'You're provoked into it. It's not like you hurt everyone. You're a healer. A fine woman.' Jane always lifts me up.

'This Luca fella? Does he stir the stomach on ya? Do you love him?' she asks.

'I don't know. I should. I'm not sure I know what true love is? Like the feelings in your books. Luca needs a woman who knows what love is. I don't fully understand it.'

Jane isn't sure what to make of that. She waits a time and then adds, 'I'm glad that he's good to you.'

Chapter 53

Dr Brady has no beard. Peering around the door, I see him against the far wall in a big mahogany bed, that is now just for himself.

He is different, like he's lost all of the bits of him that made him the man he was. His spectacles are on the dresser on the far side of the room. He's paler than a ghost and lost all his chubby cheeks that Violet says are from good livin'. They've sunk inwards, hiding his smile. The greasy hair on him is tangled in a mess at the back. His air is lacking in everything. Colour is no longer near his heart or mind and he moans into sighs until he hears the creak of the door that I move more to get into the stuffy room.

'Hullo, Molly. Welcome home, darling. Jude said you would come.'

I cross the rug on the wooden floor.

'It smells in here,' he tells me. 'Probably stale air. Could you open that window, please?' He breathes and gathers his strength to continue. 'You've not been in here much. All over the years, this was my safe place. This was where I escaped the world. Now, it's where I will die. I'll escape again.' His voice is firmer then. It is matter-of-fact with the knowledge he has from years of watching as others go over into the light. 'I told them not to send for you. No healing will cure me.'

I take his hand. We don't touch often and it feels wrong but right to touch him. He is cold to the bone. Things are bad. His fingers twist around mine. I try to ignore all the places calling for my hands on them. He wouldn't let me do any healing anyhow, I can sense it. It is pointless and we both know it. We sit a time and look at the bed, the floor, anywhere, but each other.

'I'm asking the angels and the shadows to bring you peace,' I say. 'They live with us in the dark and always try to lead us to the light.'

'You've always believed, despite all life threw at you, you've always believed.' He pulls at his nose to stop the tears. 'I'm young in the grand scheme of things but I know I must go and I am ready. Violet and Jude will need you to look after them.'

I pull away from his grasp. I am shocked by that. No-one ever asked me to look after anyone – nor anything. Bredagh took over the minding of Hull and I know the doctor and his wife have somehow found and sent Booky Mary to look after Fionn and me.

'Me? Look after Violet and Jude?'

'Yes. You. They'll be lost, when I'm gone. They'll need you.'

'I can barely look after myself. We both know I'm not the full shilling.'

'You're the fullest person I know.'

His opinion has always mattered to me. A nod, wink or ruffle of my hair, always brought me joy.

'I will miss you. Jude will miss you.'

'I'll always be close by.'

'Does Jude know what's happening?'

'We keep lots from him, don't we? He needs to know about the world and his place in it.'

'Yes.'

'Should I tell him that I am not his father? That his father isn't dying? Should we tell him that he is not ours?' A choking sob leaves and he coughs for a time to hide that he's crying. I sit on the bed and wait, watching the curtains blow in the breeze. I spy Jude coming home from school, his bag on his back. He is tall for ten years old, growing like a weed but blossoming like an ear of wheat. Cold skin meets mine again and I know the doctor wants me to tell Jude the truth for them.

'I will,' I say.

'You'll tell him? If he doesn't know, you'll give him the truth?'

'If you're sure?'

He leans back on the pillow that needs to be moved up his back more. I rise and tug at it a bit.

'It won't be long,' he tells me.

I fix his bed clothes. 'It's never bothered me to know of someone dying before.'

'That is so sad.' Dr Brady leans forward. 'Your mother's death hit you hard?'

'I killed her, that's why.'

'Darling dear, you were eight years old. Your mother died in childbirth.'

'I slowed her heart. I've been paying for it ever since.'

'There's no way you could…'

I pull over the chair, sit and watch the curtain make patterns when it moves.

'I slowed Hull's heart to let him die too. He was in pain and was dying. That makes it different. But, I wanted to kill Mammy.' I let it linger between us. 'Somehow letting Hull go was the right thing for me to do. I wasn't evil then. He needed it. It was my gift to his soul.'

'You must always remember me. Always remember the good people, the ones who love you. Help Jude find his way and become a good man. Let yourself be the woman I know you should be.'

'Stop now.'

'Let yourself have happiness. Let healing into yourself. Do you hear me now?'

'I hear you.'

There's a pounding of young footsteps up the stairs and Jude bursts into the room. His hair all blonde and floppy despite the Brylcreem he has tried to use. I can't think who he looks like. Thankfully, he is the opposite of his parents in every way. Handsome and smiling, full of laughter, despite the pain in his heart at the doctor being sick.

'Look who's home,' the doctor breathes hard. 'Isn't it great she's come to care for us all? Don't say anything yet, Molly. I'd love some tea instead. Jude always comes up straight after school to tell me about his day and what's happening in the world. Don't you, son?'

Jude is not fully listening to him, he's in my arms muffling he is glad at seeing me. A feather floats and lands in his hair. I pluck it off and put it into the pocket of my jacket and smooth down my skirt as I make my leave of them.

'We love Molly, don't we Jude?' the doctor says and winks at me.

'I'll be down in a while,' Jude squeals at my back, 'I'll bring up his tea then.'

There's a smell of onions and something meaty in Jane's kitchen as she puts on the kettle. 'I can't imagine how changed he is to you,' she says. 'He's getting weaker by the minute.'

'He is not the same man at all.'

'Violet refuses to see it. Or believe it. She never normally leaves Violet Cottage. It's beyond terrible that she can't be with him now. A young buck has taken over the doctoring in the surgery next door. I can't abide to think he'll be here and that our kind Dr Brady will be gone.' The kettle whistles and she asks, 'Do you think it will be long?'

'Not long. He wants me to tell Jude about everything.'

'I think that boy knows already, you know. I think he's got the gifts you have. I'm almost sure he does.'

My heart does a bit of a jig for a few seconds. Someone might understand me. I might not be alone in the world of knowing, yet not knowing things. 'But surely I'd see it in him?'

'You'd think you would, but maybe he is as good a play-actor as you are?' Jane winks. 'I'm telling you that boy has gifts anyhow. He does have the healing, as surely as there's a nose on my face.'

The tea-tray is ready and there is no sign of Jude to get it. I go to take it up to them and my feet on the stairs are heavy. I know that there are things to face that I won't like. All is tiring and grey in the house. Death lingers in the corners of every room. It chokes me to know it is there.

Jude is leaning into the side of the bed. He doesn't move when I enter. I can hear him sobbing.

'I've stopped his heart, Molly. I've stopped it for him.'

I put the tray on a chair and go to them. There is no need for me to ask how he did it or why. We both know.

'Violet said her goodbyes over and over. Even before you came we knew he wanted away. I just knew it. I'm so bad to him. I took his breathing away. I'm sorry. I couldn't watch his suffering any more.'

I hold Jude's slim shoulder and he pushes me off it. I can tell that he knows all the truths that have never been said out loud; Jude knows where he's from and who he is. It is all laid out there in a puddle in his mind.

'You did the right thing,' I tell my little brother. I kneel on my hunkers and move his flop of hair. 'You love him. You did this out of love. It came from the right place inside you.'

He nods and snot drips from the end of his perfect nose.

'But we mustn't tell anyone what you did. Not even Violet or Jane.'

There are drips as his head moves up and down. 'He waited until he saw you again,' Jude sobs. 'He told me that I was to look after you and Mammy now.'

'We'll need a strong man.'

'I can't, you know. I can't do very much at all. I'm only a boy really.'

'You're a fine man today, Jude Brady. You are a fine man.'

Chapter 54

'I killed him,' Jude sobs into my shoulder.

'He was ready. You took away his pain. That's a great gift. Maybe the best gift of all.'

Jude is too young, like I was, to fully understand what has happened.

'You knew deep in your belly that this was what he needed. You knew it.'

'He didn't ask me, though. He took my hand and held it on his chest.'

'That was asking. You heard his voice in your head, pleading.'

'Why didn't he ask you to do it?'

'He knew it had to be you.'

'Why?'

'It was to be someone who had pure love in them for him. Someone who had no baggage of time or worry. The greatest love of his life was you, Jude. He needed it to be you.'

'Why didn't he ask you?'

'He knew I might not do it again.'

'Again?'

I gulp, taking a glance at the dead body in the bed who was my silent, quiet rock.

'Our mother, Jude. The night you were born.'

'What about her?'

'I held my hand on her heart and let her go.'

'Did she ask you too?'

'In a way.'

'And you saved me?'

'I suppose I did. But, for a long time – maybe until this very minute, I felt like I killed her.'

'But she was hurting?'

'She was. It was the first time I felt a strong surge in my hands. I just knew what to do.'

Jude shakes his hands, understanding me.

'I think we're all put in people's paths for a reason. We can choose to help or hinder them,' I tell him. 'The angels live with us in the dark and take us to a better place.'

'Into their light.' His shoulders shake but he doesn't want to be pulled into my arms. He pushes me away and says, 'He just stopped breathing. I didn't do much. He asked me to sing to him. How could I sing? I looked at him and cried. What good was I to him at all? He brought me here to kill him. That's what I did. I killed him. All he does for me and I kill him. All he DID. I killed my lovely daddy.'

'Shhh,' I urge at him. 'You killed nobody. Whist now.'

'Jane will go mad if she knows what I did.'

'They might understand,' I whisper at him. 'But they mightn't. Dr Brady knew to have us alone with him.'

'Why did he need me to do that?' There's liquid everywhere from Jude's face, on my hands, on my clothes. 'Thou shalt not kill. I've sinned.'

'Stop that now! Does he look like a man who has been killed?'

Dr Brady's face is at peace. There is no question he is no longer in pain. The lines, wrinkles and bad colour are gone. He is almost like he was before.

'Would he ever ask you to do anything that was wrong or sinful? He trusted you and maybe this was to show you your power.'

'He always knew what to do.'

'He did.'

'What do we tell them?' Jude's shaking finger points to the floor and to downstairs and the world outside this room.

'Dr Brady died. We were here and he slipped away.'

Jude grabs at the bedclothes trying to find something. 'I can't let him go. I can't. He can't be gone?'

Jane comes in the door with a creak of the hinges. How long has she been there? Without a sound, she takes Jude by the shoulders and moves him with her back downstairs. I'm left alone with another dead body, but this time I know he loved me as deeply as I loved him.

A feather sits on the pillow next to his cheek. I take it and curl it into my pocket.

Chapter 55

I wait for Dr Brady to talk to me. Nothing. I thought there might be a glimmer of him left. But no. The curtain moves and there's only air from outside of him around me.

There is the faint crying of Jude downstairs and opening and closing of doors, but there is nothing from the best man who ever lived. I should know that the light soaks our souls into it and that Richard Brady will be in perfect peace now – why would he think of me when he's in a perfect place?

In the silence, I wait. The tone of his singing comes and I can see his smile. Around me is pipe smoke and a rasping of his beard, there's a wink, a chuck of my chin and his voice telling me, 'You are the fullest person I know.'

Those are all memories, he is gone and they are not enough.

I do often wish that my shadows had loud voices. Why can't there be a clear path? A bridge? Signs I can't miss? Why must everything be so difficult?

'Talk to me,' I whisper at his sleeping body. 'Tell me more of what's what. If it can't be loud you'll still come back to me won't you? You'll still be in my head?'

I've never wanted anyone to stay with me before. Not like this.

'This is love,' I say. 'Hull tried to teach me it too.'

'Let's sing.' I hum at him. There is nothing. No voice in my head. I should be able to hear it, but then my own earthly voice isn't strong. There is death, or is it life, that we have to break through to be together? To hear one another we have wildernesses between us now.

'I don't want to lose everyone. Who in this world will save me now? I can't look after everyone. I can't manage without knowing you are here. Without you, I am not home.'

The shadows are listening, and I hope Richard is too. A firm hand takes my shoulder.

It isn't Richard's touch.

'I'm sorry. Excuse me.' It is the 'upstart' of a young doctor from next door, coming to hold Richard's wrist and check his chest.

'I'm sorry for your loss,' is all that he mutters and shuffles away.

'We are lost from each other.' I sing and hold the hand that healed me so many times. 'You should have met Luca. He is one of the best men… like you. He loves life and is quietly a rescuer of my soul. He will have to be my home now. I just know I can't let go of my healing again. It is too precious.'

My song fills the awkwardness of Violet's screaming.

'It needs out,' I tell her. 'That anger needs gone.' I hold her back as she thumps the wall with the ball of her fist. 'I can heal most things but not dying. It doesn't need "healed" as the light takes us home.'

Jane talks on in the kitchen when we all make a circle around the table. 'Why is it that words are not enough at these times?' Her chat is full of questions about why and what and how, and the tea she makes gives us strength.

'You find the words at the right time,' I tell her, 'and we don't need food. Sit with us.'

'The doctor loved his cream buns. I have some made specially. Let's eat them.'

***

A lot of commotion starts about whether I should be about for the funeral. I intend to stay. The shadows tell me it is safe but no-one mortal believes me until word filters to Sligo about the fall of Peggy Sheeran – or Bowden, as I knew her. The woman who went missing from number 34 has not been found. However, according to the papers, witnesses have come forward to say that it is Peggy who knows of what happened and much more besides.

This helps me, but I'm still stared at and whispered about.

In the large crowds that come to pay their respects to Dr Brady there is no sign of Aunt Bredagh or my own father. The whole place is in mourning. Violet clings to me and Jude, as if we are her own blood. It makes us both glad.

'He is close by,' I tell Violet as I fix on her hat and tilt it the way she likes it to sit. The little lace trim folds down over her face a little and hides the odd tear that escapes.

'It seems that Vincent got what was coming to him,' someone says to Jane as we see the last of the mourners out the door after the tea following the service. Violet has already taken to her bed and Jude is stuffing in the biscuits off the plate into his mouth. 'That poor lass and her with a baby in tow? Poor Violet must be at her wits end.'

'Molly is married now in London,' I can hear Jane lie. 'To a fine Italian.'

'I am not! It is not my fault that Fionn has no father. But having no daddy at all is better than being lumbered with a bad one.'

'You are right there,' the woman says and leaves a red-faced Jane and me on the doorstep.

'I was saving face,' Jane admits. 'Trying to make it all better. You didn't have to make a liar out of me.'

'I'm sorry. But, there will be no more lies. I'm tired of not speaking up.'

The newspapers start arriving again after a few days of mourning. The whole place has been full of talk about the Peggy woman who took on the city of Dublin and lost. It is all there about Peggy, in black and white if I could read it, but Jude, Jane and Violet all take turns in reading me the articles and each are in the horrors about it all.

'Babies abandoned, murders, disappearances, shootings in graveyards!' Violet gasps. 'Sweet Lord divine, what were you caught up in, Molly?'

Fionn passes no heed to the happenings as usual. Jude plays with him and his toy train, on the carpet, in the parlour.

'Peggy is not as bad as it seems.'

'That's true enough. A paper doesn't refuse ink,' Jane says. 'It seems she has been committed.'

Violet tuts. 'I wouldn't wish that on anyone. That's worse than death, that is. Locked in with the lunatics.'

'They thought I should be locked away. I was too young when Mammy tried it. Luckily, the nuns were scared of my gifts and the asylum said I was just odd and that I looked okay too. What if I had a squint or something?'

'Didn't you tell me they thought you were possessed?' Violet asks.

'Maybe I was.'

'Divil the bit,' Jane says with a chuckle.

'I've the healing too,' Jude admits and I try to silence him with a look. 'I do. It is safe now to say that I'm like my sister.'

Violet goes white.

'You will always be my mammy,' Jude says to no-one in particular. 'I know where I'm from. Daddy told me before he died.'

Jane wipes her nose with the back of her hand and the silence stretches around us.

'It needed said into the air,' Jude goes on. 'It doesn't change anything. I saw Michael McCarthy in the village and at the train, a few times. Dr Brady is my father. And Violet Cottage is my home.'

Jane blows her nose and we all listen as the birds chirp in the garden.

'Is this "home"? Nothing is the same here any more.' Violet gazes out the window above the sink and pulls at the net curtain. 'Do you have to leave, Molly? If Fionn is settled here again? You'll have all of us. Is there a need for you to leave now?'

'That Peggy must have come clean about it all by now,' Jane adds. 'If there's any God at all, she will have told the truth and told them all you are innocent.'

I'm not so sure that Peggy will have sorted things but I bite my lip. 'I still cut Tommy,' I whisper at Jane.

'Do you think he'll be looking for punishment after all this time?' she asks me. 'Didn't he care for you?'

'I dunno.'

'I hope you'll stay,' Violet says.

'I wish I could go with you, Molly. I should be away from here after…' Jude stops and looks around at us.

'This place isn't the same without Richard,' Violet says to Jude. 'I understand.'

'The doctor won't be able to protect you now that he's gone. I'll try, but I'm only a boy.'

Jude is right and the angels want me to consider moving on too.

'Fionn could stay?' Violet tries but her voice trails off. 'Nothing feels right without Richard.'

'He's not far away. Isn't that what you say, Molly?' Jane asks. 'It is like when my husband passed away. I felt him watching over me when I needed him. I haven't felt it for a while.'

'Will we ask the guards what's happening once and for all?' Jude asks. 'I could ask them? There's little they can do to me. I'm only a boy, asking about my sister. I can explain I want to know what is being held over you. What do you think?'

'For a child you are a rock of sense,' Violet says, putting on her coat. 'Let's go and ask them.'

'But, what if they come looking to arrest her?' Jane gets to her feet.

'They will know she is here already with the funeral but there is no way those boys down in the village would cause us any more heartache this week. You are safe enough at the minute.' Violet's off out the door and Jude after her.

'You aren't saying much,' Jane adds as she clears the table.

'I still want to see the ocean.'

'Off to Dunmoran Strand with ya,' Jane says, clapping me on the back. 'There's nowhere nicer than there. If it's the ocean you are after there is the whole Atlantic around Sligo. And, sure, there are no beaches in London.'

As always Jane makes me laugh. All she says is true. True indeed. Where am I to go now? What will become of us?

Chapter 56

'There are no wanted posters out for you.' Jude's smile will make his face crack. 'They say the Dublin Peggy is all they need, for any crimes.'

Violet has her coat off to hang by the back door. Her face is flushed from the walking. She does drive, but daren't do it often. The doctor always had the car out and her practising was when he could take her or escape on her own. No-one sits comfortably in a car with a driving Violet Brady.

'They seem happy that all is sorted in Dublin. That Peggy Bowden is the one they want. There is no word of Tommy.'

'What had he to do with anything?' Jude asks.

'I lost my temper,' I admit. 'I lashed out at him and hurt him.'

'What kind of a man makes a woman do that?'

'Sometimes life isn't that simple. All can be fickle,' I tell Jude as he sups on the cup of milk Violet has given him. 'It changes on a whim. On gossip. On the needs of a person. One minute, I'm a criminal, on the run. Next I'm not! Tommy…'

'This means you can stay safe and sound in Sligo.'

I can't tell Violet that my angels are jumping around madly insisting that I move on again. How do I tell her? Why must I go? I don't even see a reason. Here we have a family and nice walls. London is all very well, but with the doctor gone, I can do my healing here. I can ignore the new 'upstart' in the surgery, as Jane calls him, and do my own thing. Why must I go away?

The only draw to leave is that I do miss Luca.

As if he hears me across the Irish Sea, a letter comes from Booky Mary. It's from her, but is mostly Luca's words. Oddly, Jane recognises the handwriting, calling, 'It's for you, from Mary.'

When Jane starts to read, I realise that it's true that an Italian has no shame, or at least Luca doesn't.

'Dear Molly and Fionn, Luca is here as I write and is asking me to tell you that he loves you. Before all else, I am to tell you that. I tried to explain that there is a formula to letter writing, but he is not listening. I am to write in large letters. LUCA LOVES YOU MOLLY.

'Word has reached us of the death of your dear friend, Dr Brady. We all send you our sympathies and prayers. God grant him peace and may he rest in the bosom of the angels. We hope Fionn is enjoying being back in Ireland and I am sure even in this few short weeks he has grown.

'We miss you in Cricklewood. The whole place is waiting for you to return. The grocer is annoying us all with his moans and pains and aches. Of course, my teeth are in agony since you left. The barber here says he will pull them all for me. I'm not sure I can face that until you are about to stop the bleeding and the pain of it. When might you return? Luca is asking me to ask you that as well. The dance hall is as dead as anything. They call for you to sing, I'm told, of a Saturday evening. They miss your voice.'

'Isn't this Mary the nicest woman?' Jane adds. 'Her letters have always been...'

'Always?' I ask. 'Did Dr Brady have her to spy for him?'

Jane nods, 'Don't be cross,' and she reads on. 'Luca wishes for me to tell you that a big film producer from his work heard you sing the last time you were on stage. He has asked Luca to bring you to meet him when you come back to London. Luca is very excited about this. He is jumping about the room, as I write. Does he do this all the time? His hands flying and his words are all in Italian. It is a good job that you are a quiet woman.

'He misses you terribly and tells me all the time about his deep love for you and about how he is waiting every second until you come back. I know he has not got enough saved for a wedding but he mentioned his family sending money to him. Italy is still recovering after the war, but he is trying to make a good life for you and little Fionn. There are tears in his eyes, Molly. These Italians are emotional men, aren't they? He means every word. How I wish I had a man like him who cared so much. Maybe when I get my teeth out, someone will come along? I wish you could see him now pacing the floor and wringing his hands, asking me what I am saying over and over. He tells me that he is not going to sing again without you and that he may not live or breathe properly until you come back. Lord bless us and save us all, Molly. He has it bad for you. He sure does.'

'Oh my goodness,' Jane looks up from the page. 'How romantic.'

'Is that all it says?' I'm scarlet red.

'Luca asks me to say that he will wait forever for you to marry him. That he is a good man and that you are in his soul. Also, that he will find a way to show you what love means.'

'This Italian does have it bad,' Jane chuckles and nudges me when she sees the colour of me. 'You always had a way with the men.' The laughs of her are making me more embarrassed and I hope Mary and Luca stop writing soon.

'Don't tease me,' I beg. 'It's his way. He is just being himself and he forgets that two others are reading this.'

'I don't think he cares!' Jane goes back to the page.

'We both would love to know when you are coming back. We can meet you off the truck and have things all nice here for your return. Give our regards to all in Violet Cottage. I send a kiss and cuddle to young Fionn and Luca sends all his love to you (and lust if his antics here are anything to go by).

'Lots of good wishes, Booky Mary and Luca Giovanni Romano.

'PS. This film producer is looking forward to your return too. It sounds exciting.'

'Well blow me down with the feather,' Jane breathes out and fans her face with the paper. 'I'll need to read that again, it was so much fun to read it. Better than any book.'

'Stop your teasing!'

'Wait until Violet hears that there is a man waiting on you back in London. That's one good reason for you to leave.'

'For a long time that's all I wanted. To be married and have a nice father for Fionn. I thought it would be a way to escape.'

'Ha! Marriage is an institution. It controls us. As good as my fellow was, God rest his soul, I had fuck-all freedom.'

'I know what you mean. Women come to me and when I touch them, I see their lives.'

'This Italian has it bad. Is he a bit mad in the head?'

'He just says what he thinks and feels.'

'That he does. Mary must've been dying to laugh at him.'

'She's getting used to him.'

'You do need wed. It looks bad for Fionn.'

The tea I'm drinking is cold now. Jane looks at the words. 'Film producer, eh? Cricklewood has the studios, all right. Maybe he'll make you into a movie star?'

'Will Luca let me work? Will I be able to be at the healing? Will I be able to be myself?'

'Probably not,' Jane says, rising off her seat. 'But it sounds like he'll do almost anything to keep you. I'd chance asking him. Hang on until I get my fancy pen. This is going to be an enjoyable reply.'

Chapter 57

I have sworn Jane to secrecy about the reply. But Violet asked to read Mary's letter and she took it with her out of the kitchen. She called to me from the door of the parlour, 'Molly, come sit with me.'

That usually means she wants company, rather than a talk, but once I go in she's poured a sherry and is off at full pelt.

'Richard, before he died, did many things. He was such a thoughtful man and everyone loved him. You know that, Molly, but he also had contacts all over Ireland. People who trained with him and who set up practices and consultancies in hospitals and institutions. He felt drawn to the stories in the newspapers about that woman Peggy. When he learned that you were "fond" of her, he made enquiries.' She breathes, sips and looks at me.

I'm sitting in Richard's chair rubbing the arms and listening to every word.

'I got a letter recently from the doctor in charge of the place holding Peggy. She is in a whole heap of trouble, but the man in charge believes she is not as guilty as the authorities make out. I'm not so sure myself, but these men must know their business, I suppose. He has given permission for you to visit her, if we donate to some fund they have. I said to Jane just there now that I didn't think it was a good idea to tell you. But Jane said that it might keep you here with us. If you could see this woman, you might stay and visit her. As awful as this Peggy is, Richard was led to find her for you. I should not get in the way of his wishes and plans.' Her sherry gets another sip.

I'm supposed to speak now. 'Violet, you are good at hiding the truth. I never saw this or felt it. At all! Jude gets his strength from you. He has learned how to hide from me too.' I'm not angry, but I sound a little cross. 'I'm surprised I didn't see this coming.'

'I felt that this part of your life was over and that Richard should leave well enough alone. But he wouldn't listen, of course. As usual! He wanted you to at least know where she was. I feel that she was put away for a very good reason, or for many good reasons. But sure, no-one listens to me. You had to slit your wrists to escape this woman and her hell-hole. I can't see why you'd want to visit her. But Richard thought that she wasn't what you were running from at all. Sure, that is just silly. Who else were you cutting yourself to escape from? He said that he felt you were like a daughter to her. Like me, this woman needed a second chance to… care for you properly. He said that we all make mistakes and need a second go at things. He did make me feel bad with that. Richard was good at making me feel guilty and although he never lost his temper, he had ways of telling me off.'

Her sherry is finished. The thin frame of her rises and pours two small glasses for us both. She hands one to me.

'Where is she? When can I go?'

'Do you want to?' Violet's mouth is all twisted. 'You don't have to go. Will it open a can of worms?'

'Peggy needs me.'

'Ha! When you needed Peggy, what did she do?' Her mouth relaxes. She looks into the empty fire grate. 'Yes, I see. We've all let you down at some point and need a second go at things. I see what Richard meant.'

'I let people down too.'

Violet smiles and fixes the tight bun in her hair. She has aged since Richard's death, but I wouldn't tell her that. Violet doesn't want to grow old.

'You don't let us down very often, Molly. You are so loyal.'

'Peggy is strong like you are. When I had nobody, Peggy cared for me. I don't forget that.'

'Thank you, Molly.'

'Like you, Peggy tried to better things for her family. She needed me to help her. I wasn't willing to do that. Same as with you, I was stubborn and selfish sometimes.'

'I expected you to give up your life. Your healing. That wasn't fair.'

'Peggy expected me to do things. Awful things. But we had very few choices. I understand now, looking back, what she was trying to do, but I couldn't talk much then. I couldn't tell her how I felt.'

'What things?'

'I thought my only way out was marriage. No-one was going to marry me. I was silly.'

'All women want to be married and you were thinking of Fionn.'

'Peggy tried to explain to me the ways of the world. I wouldn't listen. Like I wouldn't listen to you. I only saw that I needed Fionn back and I needed away from the darkness.'

'I didn't want you healing and making Richard look incompetent. It stung me to see an uneducated child doing so well. I'm sorry, but it did hurt me a lot. I had to listen to it everywhere I went and I let it in.'

'Peggy was the same. The other girls in the house didn't like me. They complained to her all the time. She listened in the finish. Peggy hated that she needed me. I see that now. She never really forced me to do anything and she tried to care… as best as she could.'

'You forgave me in a heartbeat. I was grateful.'

'There wasn't much to forgive. You gave me so much. Like Peggy you did your best for me. It wasn't easy.'

We both sip our sherry. I hear Fionn battering something in the kitchen and calling for Jane. There's a crash and loud curse. Both of us giggle.

'She might not want to see me. Peggy is a proud woman,' I think aloud. 'When can I go?'

'I'll write back and see.'

'Thank you, Violet. Richard would be glad to see us like this.'

'Yes, he would. Indeed he would.'

Chapter 58

My Peggy is hunched over the bare table with her hair tied back. I enter the big tiled room. She has been taken over to the convent nearby, as we're not allowed in the asylum itself. Jane is at my elbow, tugging at my sleeve. Determined she wanted to come but sorry she bothered now with the reality of it all. She was all cursing and brazen on the train, and now all meek and concerned. Violet had seen us off with Fionn waving in delight at having the cottage, Jude and Violet all to himself.

Peggy's hair is almost brown again. 'Mousey brown,' she would say in disgust. She doesn't take in that there are people coming towards her until we block her light. It comes from the large windows all around the room.

'Molly?' she whispers, her lips looking dry and her face pale. She has lost weight and looks tired but not unwell. Her air is clean and the angels are weeping that we're together again. Jane coughs and extends her hand. 'Hullo. I'm Jane O'Shea.'

Peggy stands and takes Jane's hand. 'Hello, Jane O'Shea. I like your navy hat.' Jane blushes and goes to sit on the well-used chair with the noisy metal legs. 'Look at you, Molly.'

Is she still strong despite it all? She seems it.

'I thought you might have died,' Peggy says. 'You fell off the face of the earth. They told me you were in a place like this. I cry every night thinking of us both in places... like this.'

I sit on the edge of the chair nearest me and hold on tightly to the short strap of my bag. I can't decide what Peggy is wearing. It is like a sack. A dress maybe? But it seems to have legs or is it just stuck to her? It is cold in here and she has started to shiver a little. I take off my gloves and hold them out to her as she sits too.

'She is not a talker,' Peggy says at Jane. 'Where are you from then?'

'Sligo, Mrs Sheeran.'

'And what brings you here?' She means us both, but says it to Jane. 'How come you look a damn sight better than me? Where have you been, Molly?'

'Sligo, Mrs Sheeran,' I say with a smile.

'Did you hear all about the Peggy Sheeran who was running all of Dublin and then lost it all?'

'Yes. The papers told us most of it.'

Jane starts off stammering over how the whole of Ireland was rooting for Peggy and of how great it was to see a woman doing so well. She stops when she gets to the murdering and the crimes and stumbles over her words and comes to a stop. I watch Peggy and think she is the lowest I've ever seen her. Even in the gaol, she had a confidence that soaked into me. She had enough of it to share. Now she needs some of mine as she lets the mask fall.

'I was great, all right. A fine arse I was! I dreamed too big.' She rubs her arms. They are sore. I reach out and notice there are marks on them. Long red welts. I hold them. She lets me take the soreness away and rubs them when I'm finished.

'She's a healer,' Jane says. 'Didn't you know?'

'I did not.'

'A famous one at that. She sees angels too. Don't you, Molly? Well, shadows that we all know are her angels. Are they here now?' Jane says squinting around. 'Imagine you not knowing about her gifts.'

'There is much I don't know.'

'We probably don't have long here,' I tell Peggy. Those sad eyes meet mine and she cries inside. I hear it. 'I paid them to let us in. You are being held on serious charges. They are convinced that you're one of the worst mad women in the country.'

'Don't I know it! I'm not guilty of half of it. They threw everything, bar the kitchen sink, at me!'

Jane half-laughs in nerves and fear.

'There's no way you're getting out like last time,' I tell her.

'You're talking a bit more now.'

'You need to get to Grangegorman or Portrane.'

'Why?'

'There's more chance of getting you out of there. What happened to your arms?' I ask her, knowing they slapped her for not agreeing to some sort of treatments they want to give her.

'They beat me. It's worse than the gaol. I need out. I need to be free.' Peggy grabs my hands then. 'Get your angels to loosen the locks and get me out.' She shakes me a little and laughs. It sounds a bit hollow and cruel. I can't blame her. 'You are so different. You are more *normal*.'

'Thank you.'

'But if you continue to talk about angels and shadows in here – they'll try all sorts to stop ya!'

'Molly has been through a lot too,' Jane says as the door opens and someone shouts about us having a few more minutes.

'I'm keeping the gloves,' Peggy says. 'Why did you come?'

'I want you to know that I'll make this all go away.'

Peggy shrugs and her shoulders stay there. She falls forward again onto the table. Her hands go into her hair and she moans and starts to cry. 'I killed a woman,' she sobs and Jane's hands go over her own mouth. 'I don't deserve anything. I killed that poor woman,' Peggy says.

'It was an accident. The angels tell me you didn't mean it.'

Peggy jolts up to see me. 'I shot a man through the heart.' I can tell she is looking for a confession of all the wrongs and we don't have time for that.

'He would have done the same to you, Peggy. Now listen, there is a parcel for you, too, that they've promised to give you later. Clothes, soap, cigarettes and some chocolate. I've made sure you will get it. Jane has asked around and we think we might have found some people open to helping us get you out to Portrane. St Ita's. It will take time to arrange.'

She slops back into the hard chair. 'The only way I'll get out is in a box!'

'You don't need to die, but you might need to bleed enough to get to the hospital or the infirmary here and then on to St Ita's.' I reach out and show her my healed arms. 'I've used the method before.'

Peggy's eyes are wide and they sparkle a little for the first time. Jane whispers, 'Molly heals bleeding you see.'

'We'll need to see where and what we can use to get you away and out.'

'I'll be chained to a bed no matter how near death I am. There is no way they'll let me just walk out of a hospital. No way that they'll take the likes of me, somewhere easy to get out of.'

'It will take time… and money,' I start and then Peggy laughs and she laughs on. Jane pulls at my sleeve like she wants to leave as I go on. 'I know you used to say all this to me and I didn't wait. But if you can wait, we can sort something…'

'I don't deserve out of here. I'm bad to the bone.'

'Stop that!' I tell her. 'I see the good air in people and you are full of it.'

'Pah!'

The door opens and there's a man in uniform beckoning us to leave.

'You are a good soul, Peggy. I'll be back to you. Just have patience.'

'I'm glad you came despite your silly talking. Are you well?'

'I've got Fionn.'

Peggy's head falls forward and we can hear her cry. The man moves the door and it creaks loudly.

'We've got to go,' Jane pulls on my arm. 'Coming, sir. Yes, coming.'

'Don't come back for me,' Peggy mutters. 'Don't. You are free now, little one. Free as a bird. Want more, Molly, but don't want too much. This is what it gets you.'

I hold her gloved hand but she doesn't respond and turns away from us.

'I'll be back, Peggy. Give me time. I'll be back.'

'Goodbye,' Jane says, but Peggy doesn't move and says nothing. We have to walk away. The man on the door closes us away from her with a big bang.

Chapter 59

I'm back in Dublin in a few days, looking into ways of getting Peggy out of where she is. No-one wants to talk or think of the once great Peggy Sheeran. I know not to ask out loud for what I am after. The shop on the street facing the square has changed ownership. There is no sign of Tess or any of the people I would've known. The doctor who visited number 34 seems to have disappeared himself and this makes me sad. I'm worried for him and his creaking knees and hope he spent my money wisely.

St Ita's is a grey place when I take a look at it. Lovely gardens and a laundry as well as fields for milking cows. There's a bustle about the place but the walls aren't good for me to be near. Peggy can't stay long here, if she comes at all. My impatience is high and I wish over and over that Dr Brady's brain was helping me figure this out.

Home on the train the shadows and I have a long time to think and worry. I hope that our plans will help Peggy and not make things worse.

'Maybe you shouldn't even try,' Jane whispers. 'If Violet knew she'd explode.'

'I know I'm possibly walking myself into more bother.'

'Exactly. You have Fionn and Jude to think of, never mind Violet's wrath. Someone like that Peggy might not even be grateful and where can she go? Her face is known everywhere.'

'America maybe? I've always felt a draw to the ocean.'

'How have you never been to the seaside?' Jane takes off her apron. 'Let's be brave and let Violet drive us all to the beach. It is Saturday and Jude needs away from those books and we all need the wind in our lungs.'

***

Violet finds it hard to start the engine, blaming the 'clutch and the choke' and swerves a little when she sees an oncoming car. The whole way out the road all I can see is Peggy. Fionn loves moving so fast and screeches loudly. No-one tells him to stop. There is no daddy to complain about his aching head and no mammy to hate someone else getting attention or being happier than her. Aunt Bredagh's not talking about all the work to be done in the house, or all the money we are missing by taking off an afternoon. There is no Vincent in the corners of my mind any more.

'Are you thinking of Luca?' Jane shouts back to me over the noise.

'I'm thinking of everyone.'

I've come a long way. The angels tell me that I've worked hard at talking and being brave. They tell me every day that I'm growing in strength and they are proud of me. It helps. Without them, I couldn't have survived. I still couldn't. I trust in them that they will find a way for me to be truly happy. I have to trust them, they have taken me this far.

'Look,' Jude shouts. An incline down a ragged lane appears and above the drystone walls is the sea. As far as the eye can follow into the distance – is water. I roll down the window and breathe. 'I'm back,' I tell the beautiful monster opening its mouth over and over onto the sand. 'Fionn, look it's the sea.'

Fionn and Jude build in the sand and Jane, Violet and I walk arm in arm a good distance across the shore. We don't have to speak and only occasionally mention the beauty around us and how we should come more often.

Fionn waves a sandy hand at us on our return journey but Jude is busy making a large tower. I take off my sandy shoes and dig my bare feet into the damp coarseness. The breeze is almost cold. My hair flies out behind me and I simply watch and smell the waves.

'Are you happy now?' Jane asks me.

'If Peggy…'

'Ah now she didn't worry too much about you,' Jane says. I thought she might have been more sympathetic when she saw where she was but Jane is harsh in her thinking at times. 'She didn't rescue you now did she?' she finishes.

'I miss her and Luca too.'

'Richard should be here,' Violet dabs at her nose.

'He is here,' I tell them.

A big seagull's feather floats down to land at my feet. I pick it up and dust off the sand and put it into the pocket of my coat.

The drive home is a sombre one. Fionn is sleeping with his head on the basket we didn't take anything out of as the rain came on. Jude hums a tune and watches the countryside flit past. Jane's eyes are closing but she is afraid to fully trust Violet's driving and jolts awake. I'm so gloomy and I'm not sure if it is leaving the ocean, car-sickness or something worse. It lasts in me all the way until Tuesday morning when Jane runs in with the day-old paper.

'FUCK!' she roars up the hall from the kitchen to where I'm emptying the grate in the parlour. 'Molly? LOOK!' She shakes the paper at me and pushes it under my nose. There under my nose is a photograph of Peggy from the ambassador's residence all that time ago.

'What is the matter?' I ask. 'I can't read it.'

Jane pants with the run from the gate at meeting the postman and from running to find me.

'It's Peggy,' Jane shouts. 'She has escaped! It must've happened a few days ago. This paper is old.'

I sit onto Dr Brady's favourite chair and ask Jane to read me the entire piece. There are a whole plethora of old words about how bad she is and what she did to the men of Dublin. It is near the end of that the lines I'm waiting on appear: 'When the head count was done in St Ita's in the early hours of Friday morning last, it revealed that the asylum was missing three highly dangerous individuals. Two were re-captured as they were found dancing in the Gresham Hotel, but Peggy Sheeran née Bowden is still at large. The authorities ask people to be vigilant. They have requested that the general public do not assist or provoke Ms Sheeran. They are following several lines of enquiry.'

'May the Lord keep us safe,' Jane mutters blessing herself. 'And there's more on the next page. There is to be an investigation into how she managed to get out and how no-one saw her in the Gresham or since. How did she manage it?'

'Peggy always had a way of surviving.'

'She didn't wait long on you. Thank the saints she didn't! And why couldn't she tell you?'

'I don't think she'd thought of escape, until we mentioned it.'

'YOU mentioned it! I wouldn't have the stomach for that. I wonder how she got out of that place? With all those people and walls? She is some lassie!'

Jane goes off calling for Violet to tell her the news. I watch the dust dance in the sunlight and know that Peggy is dancing somewhere pretty. It makes me happy to think that she is.

Chapter 60

Violet blows on her porridge to cool it while Fionn is making a mess of his. The tablecloth is getting a dirtying and it is paining Violet to watch it. Yet, I can't give out to Fionn. I'm far too soft and I know I am.

'No letters?' Violet asks to distract herself. 'From London?'

'No.'

'It has been a good while now since that poor lad told you of his undying love and said he wished to marry.'

'It has.'

'Molly, what did you reply? Are you staying here? I can't think of you leaving. I know you'll be trying to do the healing soon. I see you shaking your hands more and more.'

'I can wait.'

'Do you know where this Peggy woman is? Everyone thinks you do. It wasn't long after your visit. The whole place knows you went to Dublin.'

'I don't know where she is.'

Violet knows that I don't lie much and she is hoping I'm being honest now.

'I don't know where she is.' I say it again and take another slice of bread. Fionn wants one, too, and grunts at me for mine. 'I think she went over the ocean.'

'London? I hope not. You need to be free of the past!'

'I've no idea. Maybe America? New York, where the papers say her grandfather came back from?'

Violet sighs with relief then breathes deeply and asks, 'Do you want to go back to this Luca?'

'I don't know.'

'I want you to be happy of course...'

'I have to wait.'

I don't often mention my shadows or friends to Violet. She doesn't approve and tuts a bit. There is a silence that you could cut with a knife. They have told me to be patient and quiet so many times over the last few weeks. I'm not used to being quiet nowadays.

'Fionn tires you out,' I say.

Violet laughs at that and nods her greying head. 'He makes himself at home here.'

Fionn wipes butter all across the white table cloth. Violet snaps up and over to get the toast and taps his hand with a loud smack.

He doesn't cry but holds his little hand aloft at me. I kiss it better and sigh. Violet cares and only wants him to behave. I can hear and see Mammy when I go disciplining him and I stop immediately. Fionn will need a Jane and Violet if he is ever going to have manners.

'People have been calling to the front door looking for healing,' Violet grunts at me. 'I sent them into the surgery. That young lad is staying up the road but really he should be moving in here if he buys the practice. It would make sense.'

'Sell Violet Cottage?'

'It is not the same since Richard died. I see him everywhere. In his chair in the parlour. In the garden, smoking his pipe in the kitchen to make me cross and having a cream bun with Jane.'

'But where would you go?'

'I don't know. We'll have to wait and see where the angels lead us.'

I get up from my chair and curl my arms around her shoulders and hug her neck and head into me. 'I love you, Violet. I do.'

We take a few more trips to the beach and each time the weather improves. Our picnics aren't always rained upon and we have a nice time together. Jude sometimes is with his friends and prefers their company and although Violet is jealous she comes to realise that he's a growing boy. There is not much talk of the future or the past and the cottage seems glad of that.

The garden likes my hands in its soil and the flowers blossom big and full. It is when I'm dead-heading the first roses that I see a familiar head of dark hair with a cap on top of it. Luca's broad shoulders and long legs are coming around the gateway and up the lane. A small ragged suitcase is nestled under his arm and a bunch of wild flowers is in the other. He's sweating in his thick jacket and shirt and he stops to arrange himself and wipe his brow with a handkerchief.

I tingle. The rascal angels have not told me about him coming. I give out to them as I take off the dirty apron and gloves and fling them into the dirt behind me.

Violet will have seen him coming from the house. There is little that goes unnoticed. Fionn is with Jane: they took the bus to the shops in the village. Violet will be writing by the window, making last preparations for the sale of Violet Cottage. We have started to pack up some belongings and furniture and she is loving making lists of things to do. She will be watching and I may be told off for what I'm about to do.

I leap the manure pile and stride across the lawn. Luca sees me coming and sets down his case. With a jump of joy I smash into his flowers and wrap myself around his waist. His cap is knocked off as he leans over. My hands go into his sodden hair. He stinks of sweat and the long journey, but my lips meet his.

I am finally home.

He doesn't get much chance to speak or gather his thoughts. I'm eating at him like he was a cream bun. The slobbering I wasn't so keen on is very nice now.

For a breath, he buries his wet hair and face into my neck and whispers, 'I love you, Molly. I missed you.' He sets me back from him and hands me the flowers, looking past me into the garden full of blooms. 'I know you told me not to come. I know you need time, but I can't stand waiting. No more time, Luca wait.'

Violet is out on the doorstep, I can feel her eyes bore into the back of my head. Luca waves and moves to greet her. He kisses both her cheeks and doesn't even notice her thin hand. 'Oh,' she says and stiffens at his hold of her. 'It's very warm today. Luca is it?'

'Sì.'

'Come in, please,' Violet stands back and the cool of the empty hallway is good. 'Tea?' Violet asks.

When I come back from the kitchen with the tray, Luca's singing meets me in the hallway. I wait where I am stuck to the stop picturing him on stage and remembering how proud I am of him. He only sings one verse and Violet claps. Is she encouraging him to continue? Is she squealing a little?

'Molly she sing,' he tells Violet. 'She sing as beautiful as she is.'

'We heard that a film producer is interested in her singing too.'

'He wait long time now. Like me.'

'Molly has been through a lot as you know…' Violet starts and realises that Luca doesn't know very much at all. 'You know that she came here as a child? That her father beat her? That she…'

'No!' Luca's over to me in the doorway and has taken the tray. He plonks it on the good chair. 'No, Molly not speak much.' He urges me to sit next to him on the hard settee. He holds my hand and I like that. I don't let go. 'What happen?'

'A lot needs to be said. I promise to tell you later. I can speak much better now. I'm not afraid any more.'

'You were always brave. Like a lion,' Luca roars. Violet giggles. 'Fionn, is good, yes?' he asks.

'Yes. He is in the village.'

'I hear there this house is for sale?'

'We're packing up to move,' Violet says.

'Where you go?'

'I was going to get Jane to write. I just didn't know what to say,' I tell him.

'Booky Mary she learn me to write. She miss you.'

Violet must see Jane returning. She moves to get up and looks out the window, 'That idiot Jane will give herself a heart attack or pull that poor child's arm out of its socket.' Off she runs to meet them both. Luca steals a kiss and I want him to steal another but voices echo in the hall.

'Is the Italian here?' we can hear Jane ask Violet loudly. 'I saw a handsome foreigner in the village. It must be the Italian stallion. With a suitcase?' she pants. 'I thought he was headed this way. I came as fast as I could. Did she tell him yet that she'll marry him? That we are all going to London? What did I miss?'

'Whist, they'll hear you.'

Luca kisses at my hand. The glee is bouncing off the angels in the sunlight. 'Healing hands,' Luca says. 'You must always heal. Do you love me, like she says?'

'Yes, Luca Giovanni Romano. I do. My soul needs you.'

Epilogue

The nip in the breeze parts the clouds and the sun shines. I pull the collar of Fionn's little jacket up. The boat dips and sways. It rolls now and again but she steadies herself in the waves. Violet and Jude Brady, Jane O'Shea and myself, Luca and Fionn stand tall as the boat pulls out of Dublin. Our hair is blowing in the wind and we're standing waving at the shore. Jane has a new hat, Violet's got Jude by her side and I've Fionn in my arms.

'Richard is here, I can feel him,' Violet whispers into my ear and she clutches my arm. 'We will all follow your lead now, Molly. Let us try to be happy and together for as long as we breathe.'

I can't wave any more and I hand Fionn into the safe, high arms of Luca. Fionn's blonde curls are never tangled, even in the wind. I stoke his face and he shouts, 'Bye,' to no-one and everyone. Someone is playing an accordion and a fiddle joins in. The tune is lively and Jane's foot taps.

The sun warms my face and I twirl my new wedding ring on my finger. Peggy is dancing somewhere, I can hear her laughing. I touch my belly and rub the mound of love inside it. I hum to the sea and thank the angels for living with me in the darkness and for bringing me – home.

Acknowledgements

There's a special magic which brings me to write everyday. I thank and love this magic with all of my heart.

I acknowledge all those who've taken me this far along the writing road. Those who've pointed me in the right direction and brought me to this destination. Even if you're not specifically mentioned, I am grateful for every read, act or kind word.

Carmel Harrington, the Irish Times best-selling author, took me into her online writing group Imagine, Write, Inspire (IWI). Carmel has been with me from the start and from under her fairy H-mother wings, this has happened. Benji Bennet told me to write and let the rest happen. Thank you Benji.

To all the IWIers Thank you for your support, encouragement and friendship. My own new online writing group members indulgeinwriting.com, are the back-bone of my writing life. Thank you all so much for believing in me. Here's to a great 2019 for us all!

Vanessa Fox O Loughlin, who forged me on. Thank you for everything Vanessa.

Heather Norris, Mona Deery and Aishling McMahon for their unwavering support. My family and teachers through the years who gave me a love of reading and writing. Danny McCarthy, I still cannot believe you're no longer on the end of an email. Also gratitude to Ivan Mulcahy for his time and feedback in the early days.

To my writing doc, Liam Farrell - thank you for supporting me and for listening still today when I ramble on about all things #WritersWise.

To all of the contributors on our #WritersWise tweet-chats. Massive shout-out to all those who trend and chat regularly with us on #WritersWise Thursdays. To all of the other wonderful guest-hosts on our tweet-chats and on my online writing group. Huge thank you to all the literary world who give free advice and writing tips so readily.

When I needed strength there are special women out in the internet world who kept me going, Bernadene Byrne, Mary McLaughlin, Sam Hogan-Villena and all on The Extra Special Kids Facebook page.

I wouldn't have continued without the guidance from my beta-readers (especially Linda Green). The encouragement from various aspiring authors and book bloggers on social media forums/events is invaluable.

I'm forever grateful to all of the publications and literary journals who gave me readers and confidence. Also to Rachel McLaughlin, Kajsa Kinsella and Jules Mahon for allowing me onto their successful, online magazine websites to talk books or share my own writing.

Thank you to Tracy Brennan, my wonderful agent. To the team at Bloodhound Books who believe in Molly as a character and me as a writer. I cannot thank Bloodhound Books enough for making my dream come true and big thank you to my editor, proof-reader and anyone in Bloodhound who help me.

Music has a strong place in Molly's world. I acknowledge the songs, 'When Irish eyes are smiling,' 'Ava Maria'. Also 'Navvy Boots' and 'Crooked Jack' which play through my head in the Cricklewood scenes.

To all my friends, family and community who've waited patiently with me as I talked about nudges about books. For my husband Brian, you've helped me to write and to heal. I love you.